SHAUNA RICHMOND

SCREW IT!

Dedication

To Jessica, thank you for taking a chance on me and introducing my books to your store. Wishing Candlelight books every success.

To Hannah, thank you for your constant support and friendship. Cannot wait to see your work in print some day.

Craig shakes his head, still chuckling.

The bastard.

I turn, taking his measure. Like that beautiful face of his, his body is perfectly sculpted. Not so much as a shadow of fat on those abs. I think back to the cakes that I consumed earlier, feeling the slightest bit guilty for half a second before I realise that I, unlike Craig, have no one sharing my bed regularly. Who cares if I jiggle? I don't.

"Thinking about food again?"

"So what if I am?"

Damn, he knows me too well.

I locate a food parcel from the bakery and lo and behold, there is one doughnut left. My night has just improved drastically.

"Anything to eat?"

I snort. "I would think that you've had your fill."

Craig's chest presses against my back and I feel his deep voice rumble. "You're grizzly when woken up, you know that, right?" He places a chaste kiss on my cheek then turns back to search the cupboards.

"Ugh, keep those lips to yourself. I don't know where they've been."

Craig turns, pinning me with a scorching stare. He takes a step closer, then another. With each excruciatingly slow step, his joggers threaten to fall, revealing more than I bargained for. I gulp, suddenly uncomfortable. I hate it when he does this; now and then he'll look at me with that predatory stare, just to get a rise out of me. That's the problem with your best friend and roommate being drop-dead gorgeous. They can be... distracting.

Note to self; get uglier friends.

Craig steps so close that our breaths mingle.

His eyes roam over me and I feel self-conscious. My hair is a frizzy mess, and I question wearing this flimsy nightdress. I am aware that without proper support my breasts are practically knocking about my knees.

Craig leans in, ducking his head. I instantly draw in a breath and that's when he does it.

He takes a bite of my doughnut!

"I hope you choke on it!"

He chuckles lowly, a broad dimpled grin that shows the triumph in his little game of lets mess with Lottie's head.

The sugar crystals coat his perfect lower lip. I must be staring, he clears his throat, reaching over me he pours two generous servings of whisky.

"A truce," his mouth pulls to the side.

"Craig?" A muffled call comes from the floor above.

"Be right there," he calls back. Bringing his tumbler to his lips, he takes a sip then sighs. "Duty calls," he winks at me then turns for the door.

"You better keep it down," I growl.

He turns back to me, challenge sparking in his eyes. "Or what?"

"Or I'll pull her flaps over your head and smother you with them!"

Tossing his head back he laughs. "I'll behave, boss."

"You better."

"Goodnight, doll."

"Night."

A few hours later, I am sitting at breakfast, doing a spot of light reading, when the howler ambles downstairs, shocked to see me.

"Oh! I'm sorry, I didn't think anyone else was—"

"Clearly, not with the noise you were making last night."

Her perfectly plucked eyebrows shoot to her hairline, her brown eyes widening in horror, her oval face turning crimson. Not a tit to her name or an arse for that matter. She might as well be an ironing board. Fucking two backed Betty.

At least she has the decency to look embarrassed.

"You heard us?" she looks mortified.

"Everyone in a five-mile radius heard *you!*"

"I'm sorry, who are you?" She demands.

Is she serious? This is my house!

"Craig's sister," I fib.

Her eyes widen in horror.

"His other lovers are not so loud. Thank goodness that I am barren, or I would fear you would have woken the children."

"Lottie, play nice." Craig's deep voice rumbles through the house as he slowly appears behind his one-night stand.

"Oh, there is my charming brother now. How much did you pay for this one?"

Safe to say the girl has turned on her heel by now and made a beeline for the door. I noticed a tan line where her ring should be. Where on earth does he find these women?

"Oh, do say hello to that husband of yours when you see him." I imagine my voice follows her out the door like a phantom, the next thing I hear is the front door slamming shut.

"Well, that's one way to get rid of them," Craig plops himself in the chair across from me.

"I hope she was worth it."

"Worth every drop of blood that leaked from my ears," he stretches over the table, like a cat performing morning yoga. His head falls onto the hard wood and a sigh escapes him.

"Why do you do it?"

"Do what?"

"Pick up these women? I hope you wrapped up; she's probably riddled," I don't bother picking my eyes up from the book. This story just got interesting. Hello, Rhysand, my new book boyfriend.

"Am I sensing a case of the green-eyed gazongas?"

I glance up, aware that he is looking right at me with a

glint in his eye I can't quite read, "as if. You can do better—much better. She is clearly married."

I can hear the drip, drip, dripping from the coffee machine, my mug steaming between us. My book suddenly feels heavy in my hands.

"I won't be seeing her again," Craig says softly.

I watch him, there is something unreadable in his eyes, not a glint like before, no. This is different, it flashes, and it's gone. Talk about blink and you'll miss it. It's getting awkward, or maybe it's just me? Either way, I blurt out, "What? Too mouthy for you?"

Craig narrows his eyes, a stare that could split you in half. Having said that, I have lived with him for two years now and get that stare every other day. I'm immune.

"You owe me a doughnut," I grumble, my eyes flicking back to Rhys and his impressive wingspan.

"How about a dance?"

"A dance?"

"The wedding on Saturday, or has the thought vacated that pretty little head of yours?"

"Oh right, this Saturday, already?" my eyes flick to the invitation for my brother's wedding, stuck to the fridge by a Minnie Mouse magnet.

"Afraid so."

"Ugh, that means I have to shave my legs," I bite into a piece of bacon, fully aware that Craig is eyeballing my plate.

"Piss off and get your own."

"You know, I didn't get much sleep last night and I am not nearly as cantankerous as you."

"I wonder why?" I snarl. "Filthy little beast."

"Right so, I need a shower."

"You can say that again..."

That look again. *What like I'm lying?* He smells like a bordello, cheap perfume, cigarettes, and stale beer. He may have unnatural good looks and a body that belongs on billboards but by God does he smell cheap right now.

"Any requests?" Craig calls, marching from the kitchen.

"Whatever you feel like, Batman." I hear the shower running a few moments later, soon followed by Craig belting out Dolly Parton. *Great, now I'm going to have 9 to 5 stuck in my head all day!*

The phone pings and I reach across to check it. A message from Tiffy, no surprise there.

Tiffy

Can't wait 4 this weekend! We're checked in from friday. Collect you guys around 12ish if that's ok? xx

You

Yeah fine, no probs. See you then xx

I don't know what I find more surreal, the fact that my brother, the notorious womanizer is finally settling down, or the fact that Craig is going to the wedding without a date. He never has a problem finding someone, not even on short notice. He is one of those men that women just flock to.

Nick getting married though— I wish dad were still around to see this. Dad died when I was twelve of bowel cancer, Nick pretty much stepped up after that. At seventeen he was the man of the house. He has always been ridiculously protective of me but when dad died Nick got worse. He is not unreasonable by any means but anyone that wants to date me must get through him first.

Originally, Nick and Craig were roommates.

Then Nick decided that he was going travelling and Craig was stuck on rent. Luckily for him, I just got out of a toxic relationship at that time and was looking for some-where to stay. I knew Craig in passing, he was always my brother's gorgeous roommate, never did I think that I would end up living with the man. He has had a string of girlfriends since I have lived here, never anything serious.

They last about six weeks then are never seen again. I did ask him about it once, all I got back was that it just didn't work out, not the right fit. Nothing seems to ever fit exactly right with him.

After about twenty minutes with still no sign of Craig emerging from the shower, I bang on the door.

"Are you going to be long in there?"

I hear him drop something in the shower and curse it out. "Almost done. Why?"

"I need to get ready for work!"

"You can always come in and join me, plenty of room!"

Don't tempt me. He always was an unapologetic flirt.

"You couldn't handle me, Barnes!"

No response. Strange. Maybe he didn't hear me? All I hear is the sound of running water. I turn to leave when the door clicks open, steam billowing out of the bathroom like an episode of stars in their eyes. Craig appears in the doorway, that same predatory stare from last night twinkles in his grey eyes. Beads of water trickle down his chest towards a neat trail of hair cut short by his towel.

"That sounded like a challenge," his raspy voice pulls my attention away from his abs.

My eyes meet his, sunlight streaming onto the planes of his face. "Huh?"

He grins, half turning to allow me access into the bathroom. "All yours, doll." Rolling his shoulders, Craig stalks out of the bathroom, and I glance back at him, my eyes jumping from his muscular back to that firm biteable ass. With a sigh, I close the door, shed my clothes, and get ready for work.

CRAIG

*W*hy does she have to look at me like that? It's infuriating. She has to know what that does to me. Damn it. Damn guy code, damn Nick, this is all his fault. When he lived here it was cool, we got on well and still hang out— not as much now since he met the ball and chain, but still. He was a great roommate, paid the rent on time, was always up for a laugh, but failed to mention that his sister is a fucking bombshell.

When he suggested Lottie move in here in his place, I couldn't think of any objections other than I'd happily toss Nick under a bus to get to her, and I felt that might make things a little awkward. No, Nick, sorry she can't live here. Why? Because I desperately want to mount your sister. Yeah. See how that would work?

* * *

Two years prior

Taping up God knows what in one of the many boxes Nick has thrown in the corner, a strange sort of melancholy hits me. The end of an era as such. I can't believe the prick is moving out. I can't believe I haven't found a roommate yet. Yes, technically I can afford this place by myself, but if I want to afford my own place then I need a roommate so I can save up. That's the joys of being in a trade, the bank doesn't like to hand out mortgages since we can easily go belly up.

After my third failed attempt at trying to get approved, I figured I'd spend a few years saving and build my own place.

Where the hell is Nick?

He got a phone call about an hour ago and ran out the

door, saying he wouldn't be long. Yeah, right. I've sorted out these boxes for him, he can piss off if he thinks I'm packing the rest of his things.

I hear his car pull up and drop the tape, ready to go to the door and grill him, only when I get there I see her, Nick's sister. Nick's gorgeous sister. Nick's gorgeous sister who I've had a crush on since I met her.

Great. She's upset.

"Who am I killing?"

She stifles a laugh, wiping her tears away on her sleeve. "Hi, Craig."

"Are you ok?"

"I'll be fine."

"Go on upstairs for a bit, I'll get your things from the car, yeah?" Nick calls, walking for the boot of the car. Lottie looks at me for permission to go ahead, I step aside allowing her to pass.

After three trips to the car, Nick comes in and clicks the door shut.

"What happened?" I realise my tone is more demanding than questioning but right now I don't care.

"Michael," Nick grunts.

Lottie's dickhead boyfriend. I've no idea what she sees in that weasel.

"Did he touch her?"

"You think I'd be back here if he did?" stepping into the kitchen Nick flicks the kettle on, and fishes out three mugs from the presses.

I know what he means by that, if Michael hit Lottie, garda or no, Nick would be done for murder. "So?" I press.

"She was sent home from work sick, got in the door, and caught him with another woman," Nick sighs. His voice is calm, but his clenched jaw and flared nostrils show his annoyance.

"He cheated on her?" Is he fucking demented? That is

what I really want to ask. How the hell do you cheat on someone like Lottie?

"Yeah, Mom's away until tomorrow. Is it alright if Lottie stays here for the night?"

"Yeah, of course."

"Thanks, I'll eh... go and get some food in," Nick pours out a mug of hot chocolate, adds two sweeteners, and stirs. "Can you bring this up to her? I won't be long..."

"Yeah, no problem," part of me wants to point out that he said the same thing over an hour ago, but I refrain. Nick grabs his keys and leaves; the door clicks shut behind him.

I can hear Lottie's sniffing from the stairway. Nick's room is the first one at the top, beside the bathroom. We have a third room that's converted into a gym. Technically we could have got in another roommate and lowered our rent— having said that, neither of us is exactly a people person which is why we get on so well. A gym was a better investment than another roommate.

I tap lightly on the door, hearing her blowing her nose. "Lottie?"

"Yeah?" Pushing the door open, I spot her on the bed. Her eyes are red-rimmed, her nose raw and her face flushed from crying.

Offering up the mug, she takes it, muttering her thanks. She refuses to look at me.

"Want me to kill him?"

She snorts, shaking the contents in the mug. I'm glad to see a smile on her face, even if it is just a brief one. Though I am fully serious about killing the prick. I'll have no problem in burying him up the mountains somewhere for hurting her like this. I have a right mind to go over there and shatter his skull for it.

"It's my fault," she chokes out.

I can't believe my ears; I have to sit down. "Your fault?" I echo, looking at her despite her continuing to avoid my gaze.

Lottie blows on the contents of the mug then takes a sip.

"I let myself go."

"Go where?" I'm dumbfounded, completely baffled. I know the phrase well but surely I must have heard her wrong.

"That's what Michael said when I asked why— I stopped trying— he has a point."

The point being he's blind? He's an arsehole. He's getting hog-tied and thrown in the reservoir later today—

"I don't do my makeup or hair much anymore..." she continues.

"You don't need to," I insist. She doesn't! She's gorgeous without it.

Lottie starts to get all teary-eyed again and it's making my blood boil. She places her mug on the nightstand, all the while I'm establishing an alibi in my head for when the cops come knocking.

"Come here," pulling her into my chest, I feel her tears soak through the material of my shirt. Rubbing her back in circular motions, I inhale the scent from her hair. Coconut.

"I'm sorry," she chokes out.

"Don't be."

Hearing a key turning in the door, I know Nick is back. Lottie pulls back, wiping the tears away on her sleeve once again. My eyes fall to her lips, it takes everything in me not to kiss her, to tell her how absolutely stunning she is, to tell her that I'm kind of glad that Michael fucked up because he never deserved her. If she were my girl, I'd treat her like a queen. I want that, I want that more than anything. I want Lottie to myself. I want to call her mine, but I can't.

Finding myself leaning closer, I quickly change direction, my lips landing on her tear-stained cheek than her lips.

"You deserve so much better than him," I mean every word. She offers me a weak smile in thanks. Then I get up and retreat downstairs.

Nick is in the kitchen, plating up chips and burgers from the takeaway. "Hey, I was thinking..." he slides a plate and can of coke in my direction.

"A dangerous thing for you," the can hisses as I open it and take a mouthful.

"You still need someone to take my place here, right?"

He is not going where I think he is, is he?

"Yeah..."

"Lottie will need somewhere to live now," Nick stuffs two cans into his pockets along with two forks.

Shit, mayday, retreat, *retreat!*

"Yeah, but... I mean— you want her to live here?"

"What's wrong? You don't like Lottie?"

Oh, I like Lottie, I'd like her in my bed, beneath me. "It's not that. I just... I'm a guy... I thought you'd want her somewhere—" safer, where her roommate isn't going to want to mount her on a regular basis!

"Where is safer than with you? Come on, Craig, we both know if Michael is to try and come back, you would be the best person to have around her if I'm not here. I trust you with her."

Those famous last words. The words that make my heart sink to my core. Nick is a close friend; Lottie is his kid sister. No matter how much I want her, I can't touch her. Damn guy code.

"Yeah sure, if she wants to live here that is?"

"Great! I'll wait for her to calm down and talk to her about it then," Nick turns for the stairs with two plates full of food.

What the hell did I just agree to?

* * *

After two years of living with the woman, you would think I would find a flaw, something to turn me off her. Anything at all but no, she's perfect. Every other girl I've met seems to be the same, look the same, hell they even sound the same after a while. They're all tan with fake lashes, lips, hair for fuck's sake. Fake hair! I get it if their hairline is receding, or they got a bad chop in the hairdressers but come on! I brought a girl back a few weeks ago, one tug on her head and I was holding a damn smurf. Why a smurf you ask? Because her hair was fucking blue!

I saw a meme online the other day that said if you want to know what the girl you're dating looks like, bring her to a swimming pool on a first date. I know it was a joke but I'm seriously considering it.

Lottie is not like those girls, her porcelain skin, auburn hair, sea-green eyes. *Fuck.* I almost tapped out last night, had enough. I came down to call a cab for... shite... I want to say Sharon... could have been Susan? Stacey? Damn, that's embarrassing.

Anyway, I almost called the cab to send her on her way, but one look at Lottie in that silk nightdress had me raring to go. I wanted to kiss her, those perfect pink peony lips called to me and it took every ounce of strength I had not to act on it. I wanted to claim her, those lips, breasts... I could have an entire night with Lottie and not even get a chance to do half of what I want to do to her. I want to hear her moan, to watch her writhe under me, beg me not to stop. I want to watch her head tilt back while she screams my name. I want to—

My phone buzzes on the bed in front of me. Nick's name flashes up on the screen.

"Yeah?"

"Hey, man, I was just talking to Jay. He said you're coming up Friday, yeah?"

"Yeah, I think—"

"Are you only up?" I can hear beeping from a checkout in the background.

"Not long. Just out of the shower."

"Out on the tear again last night?" Nick laughs.

"Yeah, you could say that."

"Dying now?"

"Not too bad," taking a sip of lukewarm coffee that I discarded on the bedside table. I should stop thinking of Lottie when hot drinks are involved, they get cold very, very quickly.

"You'll feel that later... is Lottie there?"

"In the shower."

"Ah right, well, tell her I said hi and I'll see you on Friday, yeah?"

"Yeah, alright."

I barely hang up the phone and it goes off again.

Jay

Heard you went home with another randomer last night what were you thinking? lol

Thinking of not coming home and shagging my roommate.

You

Jealous? ;)

Putting the phone down, I quickly scan the room, looking for something to throw on. Lottie will be leaving for work soon and I've to stop off and get my chop saw back from Jay, I might as well drop her off on the way.

Don't you just love roadworks on a Sunday morning? Thankfully, Lottie shares the same twisted sense of humour as I do. Safe to say cards against humanity is one of our favourite pastimes.

"It was not that awkward," she laughs, a sound that's

like music to my ears.

"No? Top it. I dare you."

"What about Lydia's wedding. When we were looking for a parking space and I announced a little too loudly 'thank God I am not the fattest one here,' and the girl obviously heard me!"

"Ok," I laugh at the memory. "I'll give you that."

"You know what's really awkward?"

"An asphyxia wank in a batman suit."

"Oh my... Craig!" She snorts and slaps my arm. "What are you even into? No wonder you can't get a girl to stick around."

"What? You don't think I'd look good as a gimp?"

"You don't need to dress like one, you are one!"

"What's awkward?" I chuckle.

Merging lanes, I steal a glance at Lottie. Her eyes glisten and her cheeks are flushed from laughing. She has the cutest spray of freckles from her cheeks that bridge over her nose. "This conversation!"

"That's not very nice." I feel Lottie's eyes on me as I force my way in front of some road hog I dare to clip me.

"Neither is the image of you in a gimp suit."

"Touché."

"When do you finish up?"

Her eyes are burning a hole in me, I turn to face her. "I took the week off from Thursday. Gives me time to recover after this wedding."

My god, she's stunning. She smells amazing, I could devour her right now.

"Planning on drinking that much?"

"If it is anything like Lydia's then, yes, I plan on drinking that much, if not more. You may have to call ahead and book me a hospital bed."

"Why me?"

"I have no date."

"Whose fault is that."

"Yours."

"Mine!"

"I can't very well let you go to a family event alone and single, now can I? What would old Bertie Bat say?"

"Probably ask when I start collecting cats. So, what now, you're my date?"

I'll be whatever you want me to be, doll, just say the word.

"Consider me arm candy," stopping at the lights, I pull the handbrake up and offer her a megawatt smile.

"You don't think too highly of yourself, do you?"

LOTTIE

I'm busy with the prescriptions this morning— I can't be arsed with work today. Luckily, most are only one or two items so hopefully, the day goes in smooth enough. It better. I'm tired, cranky, and anxious knowing we are only a few days away from Nick's wedding.

Urgh, why do I have to be single at these things? I wouldn't mind if it were anyone else getting married but Nick, that just means I'm going to have relatives commenting on my relationship status and more than likely my appearance, giving me tips about how to get a man.

"So, Craig is your date now?" Shannon teases.

"Apparently so," I label up the box and pass it to the locum pharmacist to check off before my attention falls on Shannon. "Don't give me that look. We are just friends."

"Who date."

"It's hardly a date. We are both going, he's just hanging about so I'm not harassed and offered a basket of cats."

"Ah, the spinster starter pack," she flicks her long blonde hair from her shoulder and knuckles the touch screen. I don't know how she functions with those claws of hers, I'd poke my damn eye out.

"Exactly."

"Does Nick know?"

"That we're going? Yeah, he knows, obviously."

"About the date," Shannon presses. Honestly, this girl just doesn't give up.

"There is no date! We're just friends!"

"Sure, friends," she stretches out the word, offering me a gappy-eyed wink, "a friend you've thought of doing the horizontal mambo with for the past four years."

"Shannon!"

"What? Like I'm wrong?"

"Craig is Nick's friend," I pull down another script and

get to work pulling up the customer's file.

"Nick's hot friend."

"He has a few of those," the printer sounds and the label for Yasmin pops right out. Another person safe from unwanted pregnancy for a month— if she remembers to take the damn thing.

Shannon gets called off to deal with a customer. I love her, she is one of my best friends but thank heavens for that customer coming in. I can't take much more of her prodding.

I need coffee.

On my lunch break, I get the largest coffee I can get my hands on because Costa hasn't upped their game and made an intravenous one yet. It's a damn shame too.

Mom's name flashes on my phone screen just as I get back to the staff room.

"Hey, mom!"

"Lottie! I'm panicking! I've nothing to wear!" A damn lie the woman has a wardrobe to rival the Kardashians. A figure for it too.

"I'm sure you'll find something; you have things in the wardrobe with the tag still on."

"But I'm the mother of the groom! I need to look spectacular."

"Wanting the upstage, the bride there, are we?"

"Hey, she's got Nick! I've got no one," Mom snorts.

"Preach," I blow on the contents of my eco-friendly cup and take a sip.

"Are you going Billy-no-mates too, babe?"

"Not exactly..."

"Who?" Mom demands, seemingly perking up at the thoughts of any man, woman, or extra-terrestrial willing to be seen in public with me.

"Craig offered t—" My sentence is cut short by her cheering. "Jeez, don't sound too excited!" taking a mouthful of my blueberry muffin I wait for her to calm down.

"You and Craig? Lottie that's—"

"Not what you think, mom. We're going as friends. I think he wants to save me from another poaching after what happened at Nick's birthday last year."

Shannon bursts through the door and I wave her out. She wants to gossip while it's quiet. She can shag off. I'm in no mood.

I blame Craig and his latest conquest for me being so tired today. I wouldn't be like this if that were me in his bed last night. That will never happen though. Craig—I'm not his type. I'm not a model or influencer. I'm "cuddly" as mom would put it. It's a sweeter way of saying I'm chubby.

I could spend an hour a day just doing my makeup like the girls he dates; I could wear designer clothes and go to the gym and survive on mainly salads but that's not who I am. I'm not vegan. I tried eating clean before, lasted a day, and basically ate the wall. I love carbs and dairy. As for giving up steak, I'd hunt a cow down and slap it between two slices of bread within a fortnight. I'd never last.

My D cups need a boost, some scaffolding to hold them up. I lie down and they're under my arms, I'm sure he has never had to deal with that one before either. My point is Craig would never be interested in me in that light. I know it and for people like mom and Shannon to try and get my hopes up for the impossible is an unintentional form of cruelty.

"Are you sure nothing is going on with you two? You are awfully close."

Yeah, he's the hot unattainable guy and I'm the chubby best friend.

"Just friends, mom."

"He is a dish though; if I were twenty years younger..."

"Mom!"

"What? He has a cute tush!"

"Oh my god!" I can't even argue with her. It's that

same tush I was checking out while it was wrapped in a towel earlier!

I wrap up the conversation with mom just as Shannon comes bursting back in.

"Drinks tonight! David has Carter so we are going out!"

"But—" I protest over a mouth full of muffin.

"No buts! Momma needs a night out; you will not ruin this for me!"

"But!"

"You say but again and I'll kick you in yours!"

"Urgh, fine. Where?"

"The Abberley. Say eight o'clock? Gives us enough time to get home and ready."

"Fine."

"Good woman!"

Craig is still out when I get home. I was hoping to bum a lift off him to the pub, but a taxi will have to do. I do my makeup and straighten my hair, get dressed and head downstairs—trying not to break my neck in these heels. I shoot Craig a text to say I'm out and not to lock the door tonight, then clamber inside the taxi.

"Shots!"

"But we've already done—"

"SHOTS!" Shannon demands, the girl is guzzling the tequila like it's going out of fashion. I hate tequila, but she insists I do one with her. One is all I manage before I feel sick. It's never agreed with me. Give me sambuca or aftershock any day.

"What was that guy saying to you by the way?" Shannon slurs. She is referring to the guy out in the smoking area who refused to leave me alone for a good twenty minutes.

"He wanted to make a move, I told him I have a boyfriend."

"Craig," she cackles and takes another shot.

"No, not Craig!" I wish but no.

"Then what?"

"He told me my boyfriend was cheating on me. You know it's bad when your imaginary boyfriend is not even monogamist."

Shannon cackles then looks over my shoulder and squints. "Is that Craig?"

"Very funny!"

"No, I'm serious!"

"I'm not falling for it..." I laugh and reach for a shot of Mickey Finn. Sia, cheap thrills, comes on, and Shannon squeals.

"Let's dance!"

Shannon and I get up and start bouncing along to the beat, neither of us is Beyonce but try telling us that right now.

Dua Lipa, new rules, is next and I'm giving it socks. My hips swaying and me and Shannon are slut dropping on the dancefloor like we're about to jump on each other. I feel a pair of hands on my hips as I roll them from side to side.

"What are you doing here?" his warm breath hits my ear, causing me to gasp. Craig spins me to face him, I slide my arm around his neck, the other on the arm still holding me.

"What are you doing here?" I challenge. Why does he look so good? A simple t-shirt clings to his muscular arms, strong back, and ripped abs. The jeans— I'm guessing, are equally as flattering to that delectable tush.

He nods to Jay, Dylan, and Stephen. It looks like they had the same idea as us.

"Well, I'm with—"

"Shannon," he beams. I follow his gaze to my friend who now has her tongue down some randomers throat.

"Oh, that's the tequila..." I mumble.

"How much have you had to drink, doll?"

"Not that much," I insist.

Craig measures me with a scrutinising eye, "let's get you some water."

"No. I want to dance," hearing Ariana Grande, Into you, blasting from the DJ, I'm up. Craig attempts to grab my arm, but I dodge, instead, I reach out, grabbing the waistband of his jeans and tugging him closer. His eyes widen but he soon relaxes and begins to dance with me.

We move together in time with the beat, the space between us getting smaller with every roll of the hip until I'm practically grinding on him. This has to be the tequila.

Glancing over my shoulder, Shannon shoots me a thumbs up and I can't help but laugh.

* * *

I follow her gaze to Shannon, the two of them drunkenly giggling at each other. Then she turns back to me, her hips continue to move against me and I'm thankful it's dark in here because there is no way I'd be able to hide what's going on in my pants otherwise.

Her eyes sparkle, and my eyes fall to her lips as she bites down. Noticing me staring, Lottie licks the seam of her lips, keeping my attention on them. I find myself moving in. We're so close that our breaths mingle.

I want to kiss her. By God do I want to kiss her and I'm sure she wants me to do it.

Feeling my phone ringing in my pocket, I pull away to check it. Nick's name. *Bollocks.* He must have an alarm bell set up for shit like this.

"I've got to take this," I excuse myself and walk outside to take the call.

By last rounds, the girls are hammered. We drop Shannon home first, then Lottie and I share the taxi home. I carry her into the house, the strap on her shoes snapped when we went for the taxi, and if I left her to her own devices she would walk barefoot and probably step on broken glass or a syringe somewhere.

"I can walk," she insists.

"You can prove that when we're inside," I pull out the house keys and open the door.

Lottie heads for the stairs, falls, catches herself against the wall, all the while giggling. I'm not confident in letting her take on the staircase alone right now.

"Come on, doll," I stand behind her, nudging her forward.

"I'm fine."

She is anything but.

If I weren't acting like a barrier she would have tumbled back down by now.

Pushing her bedroom door open, she trips and falls to the bed, dragging me with her. "Oopsies!"

"No more nights out with Shannon!" I chuckle, pushing off the mattress.

She's still laughing merrily beneath me, wiggling about. Looking down I gulp, noticing her shuffling out of her jeans.

"Let's get you covered, yeah," pushing myself off the bed, I grab the duvet all the while trying not to stare. She's still in her blouse and underwear and for both of our sakes, I'm praying she keeps them on.

I bend to pull the duvet over her when her lips fuse with mine.

"I want you, Craig," Lottie is practically purring.

Oh my God! Why! Why now? Dammit to hell!

She drags me down for another desperate kiss and it takes every shred of willpower I have to tear away from her. I can't do it. Not like this.

"You better sleep that off," I mumble.

The look of hurt in her eyes kills me to see. My one chance with Lottie, the only window I'll probably ever get and I had to reject her.

CRAIG

$\mathcal{U}$rgh, kill me, kill me now. Lottie left the house this morning for work with a raging hangover and it was not the only thing that was furious. She practically took the door with her when she left.

I know she has feelings for me. If I didn't before I sure as hell do now! She thinks I rejected her because I don't want her. She's hurt, embarrassed, and looked about ready to punch my head in this morning when I asked her if she wanted a lift to work.

I tried texting her to see if she would at least try and talk to me, nothing. The texts are marked as seen— they might as well say "go fuck yourself" when I tap in to see if maybe I'd see those three dots to say she's thinking up a response.

I can't take this. If I ring her she won't pick up... hmm. I look up the store number and call in.

One of her colleagues answer and I tell them I'm Nick.
"Hello?"
Shit, she doesn't sound great.
"Hey, doll..."
"Craig," she gasps.
"I told them I was Nick. I'm sorry. You wouldn't answer my texts."
"I'm in work!"
I can hear a dick-for-brains customer in the background having a hissy fit over a generic brand of medication. "And this morning?"
"I was—"
Humiliated, homicidal, planning to move out.
"I'm sorry," I declare before she can think of anything to say. I'll take the blame for this one if I must. I don't care. I can't lose her, and if I don't fix it that's exactly what will happen.
"What?"

"We had a bit much to drink last night, I was taking advantage. Once I realised what I was doing I had to put a stop to it. Can you forgive me?"

She says nothing. I've stunned her.

"Craig... you didn't—"

"I did," I insist. *Let me take the blame for this, please.* "Forgive me?"

"There's nothing to forgive," she says lowly.

"Lottie!" I'm petrified that she's going to hang up and that will be it.

"Yeah?"

"Can..." you develop amnesia and forget about last night. "Can I pick you up from work later? We can grab dinner on the way home."

"Sure... ok, yeah."

"Six o'clock?"

"Five."

"I'll see you then," I hang up the phone, exhaling loudly. Thanks be to God. I can save this.

Stupid Nick. Stupid scruples. Stupid Bobby for raising me right. I do the right thing with her, and it took a chunk out of my ass!

"How's the head?" Jay sniggers down the phone. I'm sprawled out over the couch, exhausted. I didn't sleep much last night. Too busy cursing out the circumstances and missing my only shot with Lottie.

"Grand."

"What was going on last night with you and Lottie? Did you—"

"Nothing happened!"

"You looked pretty cosy on the dancefloor."

"What? I can't dance with a friend now?"

"If that dry humping is what you call dancing."

"Give it a rest!"

"Does she know?"

In other words, does she know that I've got feelings for her and would do almost anything to make her my girl. "No. I've never acted on it."

"Even after last night?"

"No. I rejected her last night," *stupid, stupid stupid!* Radio silence. I think I've killed him. "Jay?" No response. "You dead?"

"You rejected Lottie?" the confusion in his voice is evident. "YOU... of all people..."

"I know. Don't fucking remind me, alright!"

"Why?"

"She was drunk. You saw her, she was practically legless, I couldn't... not like that."

"Fair point. How did she take it?"

"Not well. She wouldn't even talk to me this morning. I had to pretend I was Nick just to get her on the phone."

"Will I get Tiffy to speak with her?"

"No. No, it's fine. I'll sort it. I'm collecting her after work. It gives me enough time to think of what I'm going to say."

"I can't believe she went in after last night, she must be dying."

"I'd say the majority of her shift is being spent with her head down the pot."

"Sounds about right."

"I'm going to let you go, I need to go back to bed for an hour or two."

"Yeah, go on, I'll talk to you later."

I'm sat in the van waiting for Lottie to appear. I was tempted to get her flowers, but I thought that might be a bit weird. I mean, she's my roommate. What the hell do you get your roommate after a falling out?

Just when I start to think she's snuck out the back, I see her coming from the shop. She looks exhausted. She sees me in the van and I spot a faint flush in her cheeks.

Even with the world's worst hangover and feck all sleep, she looks incredible.

"Hey, doll."

She climbs in, avoiding eye contact as she shuffles into the seat. "Hey," she glances at me, and her face turns crimson. "Craig, about last night—"

"My fault, I'm sorry..."

"We both know it wasn't you," she bites her lip. "I, umm... I drank too much. I got the wrong idea, I'm sorry," her eyes glisten with unshed tears. I can't see her like this.

Unhooking my seat belt, I scooch closer, pulling her to me. "Oh my god! What is wrong with me today?" she groans, trying to push herself away from me but I tighten my hold.

"You're tired."

"You can say that again!"

"Lottie," guiding her chin up with the tips of my fingers, I make her look at me. "You've nothing to be embarrassed about. It's just me."

"Exactly, *it's you!*"

"Lottie, as far as I'm concerned I left with the most beautiful woman in the bar last night."

"Stop blowing smoke up my ass, Craig."

"I'm not. I don't do that, you know it. If you looked like a cow I would have told you by now," an unfortunate truth. Regrettably, my mouth never did come with a filter. It's gotten me into trouble more times than I can count.

"The hot mess you had to run away from because I threw myself at you," she snorts. Wiping her eyes on her sleeve.

"Because you were drunk. I'm a lot of things, Lottie, but I'm not a pig."

"I never thought that of you."

"You'd be one of the few," I've had one too many, eh... I can't exactly call them breakups. I haven't been in a serious relationship in about ten years. Still, I've had to let my fair share of women down, not because there was anything particularly wrong with them but because no matter how nice a girl, or how pretty, or smart they were, they were never Lottie.

"What are you in the humour for?" her silken hair brushes my face and I scent coconut immediately.

"Anything I don't have to get out of the car for. I look like a train wreck," she snorts.

"Chinese? I'll order and collect."

"Sure. Thank you for—"

"Hey, I have to look after my date," buckling up, I see her lips pull to the side in a grin.

"Not planning on ditching me after last night?"

"Are you kidding me? I'm planning on payback; you'll be the one helping me nurse my hangover on Sunday."

"Is that a fact?"

"Yep. You've been warned, come prepared because this wedding will be one to remember."

And just like that, I've got her back. I might not have Lottie where I want her, but I'll settle for her being attached to my arm this weekend.

LOTTIE

There was an initial awkwardness when we got home last night that had more to do with me being mortified than anything else. I can't believe I did that. I can't believe I threw myself at him— Oh the holy mortifying shame of it!

Maybe Michael was right all along, maybe I am just kidding myself. I should stick to what I know and call it a day. Stick to the usual 9-6 of retail and guys that are actually in my league.

Three years prior.

"What you working on?" a weight settles on the end of the couch, I look up to see Michael scrutinising me with a curious eye.

"My book," I beam proudly.

"Your book?" if only I could read minds. I imagine he is screaming for a big butterfly net and tranquiliser dart. "Not this again, Char," he looks at me pithily. "There is no money in being a writer. Have you ever heard of an indie that made it big?"

"Yes, actually, E.L. James."

"Who?"

"She wrote fifty shades of grey!"

"Let's see this," Michael pulls the laptop from me, scans the page, and chuckles. "Your female protagonist is a fatty!"

"She's a size twelve! I'm the same size!"

"So, what, this is you?" he snorts. "Keep those fantasies in your head, babe. This…" he gestures to the screen then looks at me, "it's not going to happen. You haven't got what it takes."

"Says who!"

"Where is your agent? Publisher?"

"I—"

"Have been rejected several times now."

"So was J.K Rowling! Stephen King! Countless others."

He doesn't dignify that with a response, simply tosses his head back and snorts, then gets up from the couch. "I'm going for a shower," he announces, leaning over to kiss me on the forehead. "You're lucky you're cute."

What the hell?

I have a right mind to go after him and shove the laptop down his throat. The doorbell rings stopping me and my homicidal rage in its tracks.

I place my laptop on the table and go to the door.

"Morning, sunshine!"

"Craig!"

"Am I too early?"

"What? N-no, come in."

I step aside to allow him into the house, Craig is wearing his work bottoms, a black T-shirt and is carrying his tool-box.

Oh! That's right! He's putting the floors down today!

"Where do you want me?" he purrs, dropping the box on the sitting room floor.

"Huh?" I can hear the shower running upstairs, still tempted to run up and drown the bastard in it, he has me all discombobulated, prick! "Oh!, right here!"

"Are you ok, doll?"

"I'm fine, just a bit— coffee, I haven't had my coffee. Do you want some?"

"Sure, if you're offering."

I flee into the kitchen and stick on the kettle. "Two sweeteners, right?" I call back.

"Right!" Craig's voice booms from the adjoining room. I get to work making the drinks and hurry back into the room. When I get there, the blood rushes to my face. Craig is bent over the laptop, reading my book.

Oh shit! He'll probably think it's stupid, too.
I open my mouth to explain myself, but he gets there first.

"Did you write this?" his eyebrows shoot to his hairline.

"I—eh— it's a hobby. It's stupid, I know," I blush to my roots.

"Not at all. I think it's amazing, I'd never be able to write a book."

"I don't know if I can either..."

"This is really good, Lottie!"

"You think?"

"Definitely. Don't forget about us little people when you make it big," he offers me a bright smile and takes the cup of coffee from me. "Thanks, doll."

"Any time."

After we have our caffeine fix, I stay in the kitchen and let Craig get to work.

Michael comes down a short time later, barely acknowledges Craig, and sees me with the laptop.

"You want to spend more time outside rather than on the laptop, Char."

"I'm going out with mom later," I mumble, too annoyed to look at him right now.

"For lunch."

"And?" Now he has my attention.

"Try and choose the healthy option today, yeah? It won't kill you to say no to the breadbasket for once."

"What the hell is your problem?" Craig's gruff voice makes me jump, I almost forgot he was here.

"What?" Michael spins, looking rattled.

"You heard me! Who are you to get off telling her what she can and cannot eat?" Craig steps into the kitchen menacingly.

Michael laughs it off, "I was obviously joking."

"Well, I don't find it the least bit funny."

"Don't you have work to do?"

"Yeah... maybe I should pick up the hammer and start swinging," Craig growls.

Michael turns his back on Craig, "my blue shirt?"

"Upstairs in the wardrobe," I murmur.

Michael turns and I can hear him charging up the stairs within seconds.

"Why are you still with that dickhead?" Craig's jaw is tight as he stares in the direction Michael just fled in.

"He's not all bad. He's got a lot going on at work. He's stressed."

"Has he ever touched you?"

"What? No!"

"Good." Craig turns back to me, his features softening instantly. "I better get back to these floors."

"Craig," I call as soon as he turns to leave. "Thank you."

He offers me a warm smile, "any time, doll."

* * *

"Dollface?" Craig calls from the floor below. I hear the door click shut and the sound of his keys crashing on the radiator cover.

"Up here!" I jump from the bed and make my way downstairs. Craig is armed with a mini feast; he dishes up our food from the Chinese takeout and pours me a large glass of wine.

"Your pick tonight," he grins, handing me the glass.

"Hmm, Deadpool?" I suggest, taking a sip from my glass and grabbing my plate.

"Love you!" Craig grabs a can of Heineken, kicks the door of the fridge shut then grabs his plate and follows me inside.

"You love Ryan Reynolds."

"What's not to love?"

"I can't argue there."

"So, this wedding..." Craig's fork hits the plate breaking the momentary silence.

"What about it?" I shove a mouthful of noodles into my gob. I hate thinking about the wedding, I'm going to be on the receiving end of those stares—the ones you get when everyone else around you are settled down and people are wondering what the hell is wrong with you.

"Dreading it that much?" Craig snorts.

"Just a little, between Bertie, and Nick's football friends I'm afraid to see what fresh hell awaits me."

"You're afraid of a set up?"

"It's inevitable with Bertie. She will sense someone single and practically throw me at them."

"She won't do that," Craig says confidently.

"Did hell freeze over?"

"Nah, we'd know by now. Would have felt a chill."

"You know what Bertie's like. She will see that I'm alone and pounce," I wrap my noodles around my fork, my eyes drifting to the beautiful specimen on the opposite end of the couch.

"You won't be alone, doll," Craig's can hisses as he opens it and takes a gulp. "You have me."

CRAIG

*T*he bloody heat outside. Twenty-eight degrees, that's melting point for an Irish person! I'm dead. Dead. Not moving, I don't care.

"Craig!"

Piss of Jay.

"Craig!"

I'm in my happy place.

"Craig!"

"For fuck's sake, WHAT?"

"What the hell crawled up your arse and died today?" he stares at me with his big amber eyes, he looks like a puppy. It means he wants something. I don't even want to know. The last time he looked at me like that, he set me up with one of Tiffy's mates. I took one for the team that night. Battle-axe Barbara, "but you can call me Barbie," yeah, right, if Barbie looked like Pete Burns on crack. The only thing real about her was her Mariah Carey attitude. Apparently, I was such a gentleman for paying for dinner and her taxi home, little did she know I was paying to get her the hell away from me.

"Unless your next words are working air-conditioning, piss off," I stomp out my smoke and head back to work.

"So, I was thinking... Tiffy has this work do tomorrow night and—"

"I'd rather have a rottweiler play fetch with my balls."

"You don't even know what I was going to say!" Jay protests.

"No?" I spin to face him, feeling the sweat streaming down my face. "What's its name this time? I've already met Cockeyed Courtney, Man hands Margaret, and Slip 'n slide Sandra who else are you going to throw at me?"

Jay tries and fails to fight back a laugh.

"Ask Dylan. I'm not doing it," I spin for the house.

"But!"

I can feel my phone vibrating in my pocket, Lottie's name flashes on the screen. "Hey, doll!"

"Hey, are you busy?"

"No, not at all. What's up?" I catch Jay making kissy faces to Dylan, he doesn't think I see him. I respond by rooting him up the ass. That steel-toed boot earned me a yelp and a look Medusa would be envious of.

Two years prior.

Nick's mom wanted some work done in the house, so Nick offered up my services. I've been working here all week. First, it was her new kitchen, then her stairs, creating a new banister and putting up panelling, finally onto the floors now.

I'm here earlier than expected, Kim is away and gave me the key to let myself in and out. I've got a date tonight so I figure if I start early enough, I can finish early and head home to get showered and dressed before I've to meet Amy for dinner.

Hearing a thud against the front door, I go to investigate, making it to the hallway, decorated with family pictures from all age ranges. Everything from Nick and Lottie as toddlers to Nick's birthday last month. I'm even in a few.

The door cracks open and I hear heels on the new wooden floor.

"Lottie?"

"Craig!"

I glance back at the clock in the kitchen, six-thirty. What the hell is she doing here so early? Lottie takes a step toward me and stumbles.

"I got you!"

"Shit! Sorry!"

"You're fine," I can smell the alcohol from her. She must have been out last night. Taking a good look at her once she has steadied herself, I can see her mascara has run, her eyes are bloodshot, where the hell has she been? "Are you ok, doll?"

"I'm fine!" she tries to hurry into the kitchen, stumbles, and I catch her again.

"Come on," I pick her up and carry her inside, placing her down on the dining chair. "Let's get you out of these death traps before you snap your ankle," I help her with the straps on her shoes and place them under the table, somewhere she cannot fall over them.

"Did something happen with you and Michael?" I ask after a minute of awkward silence.

"No, I— I guess I drank too much," she sniffs.

"What happened?"

"We were out in The Academy with some of his work friends, everything was fine. He tapped me on the shoulder and told me we were going home, and I went to the table and said goodbye to everyone," tears begin streaming down her face.

"Then what happened?" I press, still hunkered down in front of her, trying to gaze up at her but she keeps moving her head, trying to avoid showing me how upset she is.

"Mike said he was going to the bathroom, so I waited at the stairs. He... he never came back. I must have missed him."

"How did you get here?" I ask, noticing she has no jacket, phone, keys, nothing. She must have used the spare key outside to let herself in.

"I walked back to the apartment..." she begins. My blood is already boiling.

"But when I got there, Mike never answered and I couldn't ring because I forgot my phone, he had it. Along with my money, I didn't know what else to do so I came here."

I'm going to murder that prick. I'm going to get a hot glue gun to his bollocks and light the fucker up! I'm going to—

"Shh, it's ok. It's ok. You're safe now," I pull her down to me, holding her close as she sobs uncontrollably.

"I'm sorry!" she squeaks, hiding her face in her hands.

"Hey, doll, look at me," I frame her face in my hands, she hesitantly glances up at me. "You have nothing to be sorry about, ok?"

She nods, wipes her eyes then pushes herself to her feet. "I should try and get some sleep."

"I'll help you upstairs," I guide her up to Kim's bedroom and help her to bed. Closing the door behind me before shooting off a text to Nick to let him know what's happened.

A few hours later, Lottie comes downstairs looking a little less worse for wear.

"Hey, doll!"

"Hey," she yawns and stretches out her limbs, "the house looks beautiful," she smiles warmly, admiring the new stairs and rails.

"Thanks. How are you feeling now?"

"Tired, embarrassed. Sorry you had to see me like that."

"Don't be."

Lottie runs her hand over the rose designs on the panelling, "how do you do it?"

"Do what?"

"Take something so broken and make it look new?"

"Nothing's ever really broken."

"You think?" her eyes sparkle back at me through her mass of unruly hair.

"With most things, a bit of sanding down and a lick of paint will make them look brand new again."

"And what about the other bits that are not so easily

repaired?" she asks, taking the final step from the stairs into the hallway.

"Those are the best bits. Some pieces have been neglected so much that they'll never be what they once were, but with some patience and some TLC, they become something new. I find those are the ones that turn out to be even better than what they were originally."

"Wow, that was beautiful," her smile widens. "So, erm... you must be hungry, I can order us some dinner, my treat?"

I glance at the clock. If I don't leave soon I'm going to be late. My eyes flit back to Lottie who is staring at me waiting for an answer.

"I'm sorry, you must have plans—"

"No. No plans!"

"Are you sure?"

No. I find myself grinning back at her, "positive."

"Great, I'll order out then? We can find something on Netflix if you want. Or you probably just want to go home to bed?"

"No, Netflix sounds good. It was pretty much my plan for the night anyway," oh my God! What the hell am I doing? Ok, it's half four, if I leave by six I can still make it home, change and meet Amy. I got this. It'll be fine.

"No way!" Lottie laughs hysterically. "Jay of all people?"

"Yep."

"But he's a big teddy bear!"

"What can I say, he has a grizzly side," I shrug.

"Assault though, I never would have thought," she shakes her head and takes a sip of her drink.

"In his defence the guy had it coming. He came at Jay with a broken bottle, so Jay broke his wrist."

"And the other time?"

"Meh," I shrug again, smiling at how interested she

seems to be in my past. "He had it hard growing up. He was angry and young. We both were."

"Each other's ride or die?"

"Something like that," I nod, feeling my phone buzzing in my pocket. I pull it out to see a text from Amy. I don't open it immediately, instead, my eyes flick to the clock. 18.20. *Crap.* Even if I leave now I'm going to be late. I glance back to Lottie who has turned her attention back to the T.V, despite the messy hair, her mom's dressing gown, and makeup still lingering from the night before, she still looks breathtakingly beautiful.

"Run bitch, ruuuuun!" Lottie squeals at the T.V as another "teenage" damsel tries to escape a knife-wielding maniac. It's been so easy with her today. Too easy.

I tap out a quick text to Amy saying I got held up at work and I'll need to take a rain check. I have no intention of leaving Lottie now. I knew that as soon as she offered up an evening together, I guess I hoped that I would show some willpower and leave. Turns out the only thing to piss off was my resolve.

* * *

"I'm off earlier tonight so I can pick up dinner if you want?" Lottie's voice pulls me back to the here and now.

"Yeah, sure... if you don't mind?"

"Of course not! Steak sounds good to you?" I can hear the chatter of people in the background, she must be in costa for her caffeine fix.

"Yeah, sounds great! Do you need me to bring anything home?"

"No. I think I have everything."

"Great, I'll be home around eight if that's ok?"

"Perfect! I'm off at six, it gives me enough time to get home and get dinner prepped."

"Grand, see you then, doll!"

We finished up a little earlier today, I pull up to the house at half seven and hear the music blaring as I approach the door.

I crack the door open and step in, purposefully trying to make as little noise as possible. I'm greeted by the Thong Song booming out of the kitchen and catch a glimpse of Lottie sliding across the floor to the press where we keep the pots and pans. She bends down and twerks— badly. I bite my lip to stop laughing. She has no idea I'm home, and I want to take these few seconds to admire her.

She comes back up, armed with the pasta strainer and I instantly know we are having spaghetti bolognese tonight, a glance at the garlic bread cooking in the oven confirms it. She obviously was not impressed with the cuts of steak in the supermarket.

Lottie slides back to the hob, bringing the pasta down to a simmer before it boils over. She whips her head back and forth, shimmying in place. This is the side of herself I wish she would show more often. This goofy, confident side that she is afraid of people seeing. I step back to the hallway, open the door, and call out, "Dollface."

"In here!" she calls, stepping out of the kitchen to greet me. "You're back early."

"I'm not disturbing you am I?"

"Not at all! Dinner's almost ready," Lottie spins back for the kitchen.

"So, I meant to ask... what happened to that guy Peter?"

"Parker," she corrects.

"Yeah, Spidey boy. You were seeing him for a while right?" I hated the little shit. Thought he was above everyone because his daddy is a doctor. Someone ought to tell the good doc that he needs chlorine in that gene pool.

"We weren't compatible," Lottie shrugs. She went out with him for about two months, so it wasn't the personality that sent her running—he was shit in the sack, wasn't he? I grin like a Cheshire cat.

"What are you smiling at?" she shoots me a playful grin of her own.

"Nothing, I just feel sorry for the guy."

"Why is that?"

"Impotence at his age. I suppose he can always buy a strap on."

Lottie throws her head back laughing. I pull out the dining chair, watching the way her smile reaches her sparkling eyes. The dusting of freckles across her cheeks, the crinkle of her nose when she laughs. She's stunning.

"Parker was not impotent," she says once she catches her breath.

"No? Micro penis?"

"Craig!"

"Not compatible after that long means he did something wrong in the sack, doll," couldn't have been the wrong hole. That's usually frowned upon but not a dumpable offence. "What was it? He had a weird kink, he sneezed when he came, he was into pegging wasn't he?"

"It..." she breaks off laughing again. Lottie serves up the pasta and turns for the sauce.

I think back on her little time with him. He stayed over twice; three times max that I remember. Suddenly a lightbulb goes off. A eureka moment of sorts. My grin grows wider. "He couldn't get you off, could he?"

"Craig!"

"That's it, isn't it!"

Lottie carries the plates to the table; her cheeks are flushed, and I know I'm right.

"If you have to ask..."

I bet that's what she said when he asked if it was good for her.

"What about you and, well... any of them?" Lottie twirls the pasta around her fork before taking a bite.

"In order?" I take a bite and think over the last handful

of girls that I've dated. "Gold digger, gold digger, narcissist, masochist, gold digger, thick as two planks."

"How thick are we talking?" Lottie cocks an eyebrow.

"I made a joke about Sherlock Holmes, and she asked me who he is."

Lottie stops dead in her tracks, fork paused in mid-air. "Wow."

"Yep, but don't feel too sorry for me, doll. I have my arm candy the wedding," I wink at her and notice her cheeks flush. I want so badly to stretch over and kiss her.

I can't take much more of this. I can't keep staying away from her, I can't not kiss her. I'll get this weekend over with, let Nick have his day and then I'm getting my girl. I've no idea how I'm going to do it yet, but I'll figure it out.

THE WEDDING

A date! A date with Craig Barnes. I know it's not an actual date, he's there for moral support, to keep my suffocating relatives at bay about me being single and pushing thirty. Yet, I can't help the butterflies doing laps around my stomach at the thought. That delicious man attached to my arm for the night.

I can't help thinking of what he said the other day, that he pulled away because I was drunk (which I was, I was well past drunk) he didn't want to take advantage. I can't help but find him more attractive because of that. He never said he wasn't interested, in fact, he said I was beautiful, didn't he?

Friends, Lottie, friends. Nothing can ever come of it. Sex complicates things as it is— oh, who am I kidding, he does not see me in that light. I'm friend-zoned for life. I can pretend though, right? I can act like he finds me desirable for just one day.

My bank account officially hates me, I had a dress. A lovely dress, but knowing Craig is to be with me for the day I suddenly decided I hated it and went out to buy another. Adding on hair and makeup costs to it does not help. I will be broke next month but who cares.

I came back to the house while Craig was in the shower, he is yet to see me. *Oh God, why am I so nervous?*

I slide on my beautiful white risqué dress. The off the shoulder sleeves sit halfway between my shoulders and elbows. The gown is cut dangerously low, and it hugs me in all the right places. My hair is loosely twisted into a low chignon with white and blue flowers woven in. My eyes are dusted in neutral browns and golds.

A bit much for pre-wedding drinks perhaps? Who cares? I have an even more enticing dress for tomorrow.

"Lottie, you ready?" Craig calls.

"Be right out!"

I hear Craig and Jason talking downstairs. I'm assuming Jason is being loaded up like a mule considering the grunts and colourful words exchanged as he leaves.

"Lottie!" Craig calls again.

Taking a deep breath to steady my nerves, I open the door and do my best to look confident.

"No need to shout, I can hear you."

He turns to see me coming and staggers back. A noise somewhere between a gasp and a moan escapes him.

I can feel my cheeks heat under his darkened gaze.

"You look... beautiful."

"Thank you," I imagine that I'm blushing to my roots.

* * *

She had to wear that dress. She had to wear something to draw attention to those tits. How am I going to keep my eyes off her? Thank God I was holding the jacket of my suit when I saw her, I imagine my reaction would have been harder to hide. Sitting in the car across from her while I'm practically tenting in my pants doesn't help.

It's fine, we will get to the hotel, check-in and I can put some distance in.

"How long of a drive?" Lottie asks, rummaging in her bag, looking for god knows what, I lean forward, getting a quick glimpse down her dress.

"About three hours," Jason replies.

Tiffy is in the front seat, fingers laced with Jay's as he continues to shift gear while we enter the motorway.

"You know what would be so good right now?" Lottie asks.

That dress on my bedroom floor.

"What's that?" Tiffy looks back, grinning like a Cheshire cat. Clearly had a quickie with Jay before they came for us.

"Ice-cream."

"When we pull off the motorway I'll stop at the services," Jay offers to the girls' delight.

* * *

I really wanted ice cream, but they only had the machine kind and I'm not risking spilling anything on this dress! I spy a Roundtree ice pop and take that to the till instead. Craig and Jason have loaded themselves up with snacks for the next half of the trip.

"You went all out on that dress," Tiffy smirks.

"It's a nice dress."

"I'm not denying it. I also know that the builders over there getting their chicken fillet rolls are not the only ones approving of your chosen attire," she nods to the window.

The guys are walking back to the car, Craig gives a glance in my direction then continues to look ahead of him.

"Don't be daft. He's probably just surprised that I don't look homeless for once."

* * *

Sweet baby Josephine and all that is holy, is she doing this on purpose? Ice-cream! She distinctly said she wanted ice cream! But nooooo, instead, she chose a phallic-shaped ice-lolly and is sucking the ever-loving hell out of it, inches from where I sit!

How much of that can she fit in her mouth? No! Stop! Shit, I'm starting to tent again.

"Are we there yet?"

"What's the matter, Craig? Bored already?" Tiffy teases.

"I just... not used to being the passenger."

"Wanna trade places?" Jay chuckles.

Yeah, with that fucking ice-lolly!

"Nah, I'm good, just turn on something decent will you?"

For the rest of the drive, Jay has the radio on, the girls belt out dancing queen, and of course, Bruno Mars marry you. It would help if one of them had a note in their head, but I won't hold that against them.

We arrive at the hotel and check-in. Tiffy and Jay are all over each other at the desk while I wait behind Lottie to get my room key.

"That can't be right?" Lottie argues.

"What's wrong?"

"They've mixed up the reservations. Put us in the same room," her brow furrows.

"What?"

"I'm sorry, I don't know what happened..." the flustered receptionist explains, she continues to tap away on the keyboard as if searching for an answer to how this happened.

"It's fine, I'll just take a different room now..."

"We're fully booked out."

Christ on a bike! Is this actually happening?

"What do you want to do?" Lottie looks at me with anxious eyes. "We could book another hotel?"

"No. That will take away from the entire weekend, everything is happening here and if this place is booked out, I imagine the closest hotels aren't much better for availability."

"I'm sorry for the mix-up. We can offer complimentary food and drink in place of the room."

Lottie looks at me through lowered lashes and all I want to do is slam her against the reception desk and tear the dress from her.

"Free food," her eyes sparkle.

"Free drink," I nod. "Sold."

Now the real question is, how am I going to survive an

entire weekend with her in the same room as me? At least there should be two beds, right?

* * *

"How do you want to work this?" Craig asks as we stare blankly at the double bed in the middle of the room.

The room itself is beautifully decorated. The bed is bigger than the standard double you find in most rooms. We have great space in here, too.

Maybe this is a sign? I mean, he offered to be my date, so to speak. We got put in the same room, with one bed. Is it just wishful thinking that the universe is permitting me to sleep with my roommate? Would it be so terrible if we did? I mean, we are friends, we both trust and respect each other. I know I know these things never work out but maybe, possibly, with a bit of liquid courage... could a drunken tryst be that bad?

"I could take the couch," Craig offers.

I glance at the couch by the window, it's tiny. His six-foot-four athletic frame would not fit on that without him turning into a damn contortionist.

"No. I mean, we could just... share? If you're comfortable with it that is. I mean, I'd share with Tiffy or Shannon, why should you be any different, right?"

"Right, right," he shuffles back and forth on his feet for a minute. His cinnamon brown hair falling in front of his eyes.

Reaching out I brush the strands away, his grey eyes sparkling back at me. That predatory stare again. The one that causes my cheeks to flush and my heart to start racing as soon as he looks at me.

"Free drinks?" I squeak.

"Please."

The barbecue and pre-wedding drinks don't start until five

but given our current situation, we figured we would get the drop on everyone else.

Cocktails are two for one for everyone else but free for me, so safe to say the forty-five-minute head start we had seen me well and truly hammered by the time the stragglers arrived at seven. I don't care. Free drinks. Free!

I don't know whose idea the tray of sambuca was but it's all free, I'm not saying no. Everyone gets sambuca. I'm turning into Oprah here, lashing the shots out.

Safe to say Craig is feeling the same way when it comes to our free bar. Beer, whisky, Jager bombs, you name it, he's drinking it.

"Jaysus the tits on yer one!" he announces, catching sight of a busty bridesmaid.

"No bringing anyone back to the room, Barnes."

"Me? I would never! The only one coming to bed with me tonight, love, is you. And yer tiddies are much nicer!"

"Thanks for the compliment!"

"How much have you two had to drink?" Jay chuckles, watching me use Craig's chest to steady myself, his arm slung around me while he sings take a chance on me at the top of his lungs.

"Clearly not enough!" Craig calls over the cackling bridesmaids. I feel him pull me in closer, "Cause I've got, so much that I wanna do, when I dream I'm alone with you, it's magic!"

I can't help but sing back to him, "you want me to leave it there."

"Afraid of a love affair, but I think you know..."

"That I can't let g—"

"Get a room!" Jay chuckles over the howling.

"We got one!" Craig yells triumphantly, his hand slips slowly, fingertips grazing my side, sending a delightful shiver through me. His hand abruptly stops, and he pulls away to go to the bar.

* * *

Drinks! So many drinks, I don't know when we moved away from Jay but suddenly, I'm on the dancefloor with Lottie, guiding her arm to my shoulder. I don't know what I'm doing, I just need to touch her. Need to be close to her. Pressing my forehead to hers, we spin in a pirouette, Jay and Tiffy have paired up beside us, spinning and dipping their way along to the music. Lottie places both hands on my neck and sways her hips to the rhythm.

She looks gorgeous, I know I'm not the only one here to notice her. How she is still single is beyond me. If she were not my roommate, I would have snatched her up by now. God, I want her so badly. She looks up at me, those sea-green eyes sparkling and I'm enchanted.

We move as one, hips together, fingers laced as the DJ starts playing songs from dirty dancing. I see it as an excuse to get closer, whirling her outwardly then slowly drawing her in.

The music stops, I catch Nick eyeballing us suspiciously and I find myself in desperate need of another drink. I hate bro code.

* * *

"I think you've had enough," Tiffy giggles when I debate ordering another drink. She's probably right. I don't want to be in bits tomorrow for Nick's wedding. Instead of ordering another sex on the beach, I order a pint of water and chug. When I'm done, I decide to call it an early night.

Tracking Craig down is not hard, he is at the other end of the bar. I ask for the room key, but he insists on walking me back to the room, a wise choice considering as soon as we get back I have trouble taking off my shoes.

Sitting on the bed, I toss my leg up onto Craig's

shoulder for him to help me. My heels hit the floor with a thud, and I stand.

We are so close that we can share the same breath.

Maybe it's the alcohol or the way he is looking at me right now, whatever it is, I pull my arm to the zipper on the back of my dress and tug.

He looks at me with that predatory glint in his eye and pounces, teasing my lips apart, he gently sucks and grazes my bottom lip before dominating my mouth with his tongue. He tastes deliciously sweet, most likely from that honey JD he's been ordering for most of the night.

"Lottie," he whispers, trailing soft pecks from my jaw to my collar bone. "I better close the door," Craig pulls away, turning for the door to our room that is ajar, allowing the light from the hallway to spill into the room. With a gentle nudge of his foot, the door clicks shut.

* * *

Waking up to the blinding sun beaming on my face, I groan. My mouth feels like a desert and my head is pounding. I can't even open my eyes; my lids feel like they've been glued shut. Thank God the wedding is not until three. Gives me some time to recover. An open bar sounded like a great idea until we took full advantage of it. I wonder how Lottie is— images of last night flash before my eyes. Her lips on mine, Lottie beneath me, clawing at my back—

Did I dream that? Did that happen? Did we?

I peel my eyes open and peer around the room. No Lottie in sight. She's gone. She's gone and I'm naked. I spy her dress on the floor, exactly where we left it last night. *Oh my God,* it did happen, we actually—

My already parched mouth is vacant of all forms of fluid. I should be ecstatic; I've wanted this for so long. Wanted her for so long. Last night from the parts I remember was fantastic. We were great together.

How could I be so stupid? I not only slept with my roommate and friend... I never used a condom.

Before I have time to think, my phone pings.

Jay

You want to get your ass down here before the girls demolish the buffet.

You

Be down in a minute

Ok, ok... she obviously went to join them for breakfast. I glance at the clock to see it's just gone ten. The girls are booked in the salon for twelve, Lottie is anyway.

Right, act natural.

Hey, Nicky, what's that? No, I didn't have drunken mind-blowing sex with your sister last night.

Should I shower first? Or go straight down to Lottie, rip the bandage off so to speak. Shower... Lottie... Shower... Lottie in the shower... No stop! If it were not for the gutter my mind would be homeless.

Right pants, pants would be a great start. Where the hell are they?

I eventually find some clothes that do not smell like stale alcohol and make my way downstairs. My head is banging. I should have taken a lifeline before I start drinking. I wonder if there is a pharmacy nearby.

Nick, Jason, Tiffy, old Bertie bat, and Lottie are sitting around a table. Inhaling deeply to steady my nerves, or possibly my stomach, I move in.

"Ah, there he is," Nick declares when he spots me approaching.

"The free bar proved too much for you, eh?" Jason sniggers.

"Something like that," I lower myself into the only available seat, on the opposite end of the table from Lottie, shit!

"Are you down here long?" I direct the question at Lottie, but of course, old Bertie has to jump in and answer for her. "Not long at all, about what? Half an hour, max."

Lottie gives a slight nod, her cheeks flush. Bertie is scrutinising the pancake stack in front of her niece.

"You want to ease up on the carbs, girl, if you want to catch yourself a man."

Is she for real? Seriously!

"Because I'm really going to find one at a family event," Lottie growls.

"Not if you keep eating junk like that, you never know who might be at one of these things."

"Well, I think Lottie is beautiful the way she is," Tiffy declares, flicking her hair defiantly.

Too right!

The waitress comes over to take my order, I can't decide what I want. Nothing on the menu is grabbing my attention. I am trying so hard to not excessively stare at Lottie. Panicking, I order the pancakes, the pastry basket, and the full fry up.

"Hungry?" Nick chuckles.

"Ravenous..." I find Lottie's eyes immediately. They sparkle back at me from across the table and I want nothing more than to kiss her. To hold her. I thought that if I were lucky enough to be with her even just once, that I could get her out of my system. That it was nothing more than lust. That it was the red button that I'm not supposed to push but once I did I would just... I don't know... walk away? That things could go back to normal, but no. After having Lottie, kissing her, tasting her, hearing her call my name, I'm hooked. Addicted. I need another hit.

"Is there a pharmacy nearby?" Lottie asks, "My head is killing me."

"Yeah, there is one just down the road about ten minutes' walk," Nick offers.

"I'll go with you," the words spill from my mouth before I can second guess myself. "I was thinking of picking up some lifeline before the wedding."

"If the way you were drinking last night is anything to go by, you'll need it!" Jason chuckles.

After breakfast, I have to go back to the room for my wallet. Lottie follows in silence. Does she regret last night?

"Are you on the pill?" *What? That is what you open with? Seriously? What kind of question is that?*

Lottie smiles weakly, her voice uncharacteristically low. "No. I haven't... needed it for a while now. It's why I want to go to the pharmacy."

"Ah, right." Shit, this is awkward. Why is this awkward?

"I don't regret it," I say at the very same time as Lottie speaks. "I'm sorry, I was drunk—"

"What?" We ask in unison.

"You don't?"

"No. Do you?"

She takes a minute to answer, it feels more like hours. "No. I don't. But we're—"

"Friends. Roommates."

"That and you're Nick's friend, too."

"I know," I rub around my eyes, this headache is relentless. "Though, I did think we made a good pair last night."

She giggles, blushing to her roots when she spots her discarded dress on the floor. "I can't argue there."

She looks up at me through lowered lashes and I can't help myself, I move in. I claim those perfect pink lips with my own, Lottie parts her lips, granting me access. Our tongues intertwine. Her hands are on me, running through my hair, pulling me closer.

With a throaty growl, my hands run down the backs of her legs and hoist her up, hooking her legs around my waist.

We slam into the wall. My hands are all over her, exploring her curves, moulding her breasts. Lottie's breathing comes out in laboured pants. I tilt my head upwards for another desperate kiss. Lottie hikes up my shirt, raking her nails across my back, drawing out a hiss. She reaches between us, palming the hard evidence of my desire for her.

"Fuck, Lottie..." nibbling on the whorl of her ear, she moans, sliding her hand under the band of my trousers, I feel her grip me. Her hand slides down my length then back up.

I slam her hands against the wall, kissing and nipping at her neck, wanting nothing more than to take her here and now.

"We can't. Not without protection," I groan into her neck. Kissing her once more before I lower her to the ground and step away, clearly frustrated. I've never gone without a condom until last night. I've never been so drunk or eager to be with someone that I forgot all about one. Lottie is different, it's like I can't control myself with her. "We're stuck here for the weekend, right? Like this? Sharing a room."

"Until Monday," she nods. "Why?"

"We go to the pharmacy, get you the morning-after pill, and I'll get us some protection," I step closer, framing her face in my hands. "I won't be able to keep my hands off you this weekend, not after last night, Lottie. I have to have you again."

"We can't."

"We already have, doll."

"Just this weekend?" she asks, a wicked gleam in those sea-green eyes.

"Just this weekend. Get it out of our systems."

"Today barely counts, you know. Nick's wedding and all. We won't be able to do anything."

"That sounds like a challenge."

She smiles warmly and I kiss her again. I can't help it. I'm drawn to those lips.

After adjusting myself and grabbing my wallet we head for the pharmacy.

While Lottie's in the consultation room with the pharmacist, I make my way to the condoms. I pick up the three-pack then look at the room Lottie's in. If I only get her for the next two days I'm going to make it count, wedding or no. Three won't cut it, I pick up the twelve and again think about last night. Think about ten minutes ago back in the room, the things I want to do to that girl. The things I plan to do to that girl. Hmm... I look back at the shelves, buy one get one half price, two twelve-packs it is. Making my way to the counter just as Lottie is coming out with the pharmacist. Protection, and a family-sized box of painkillers because my God, my head is banging to what I can only assume is my own death march.

I'm supposed to be here for a wedding. A friend's wedding. I feel like I'm having an affair, cheating on Nick with his sister. I shouldn't do this; I should show some sort of self-control. I glance back at Lottie and all my resolve is gone out the window. Sorry, Nick.

LOTTIE

*W*hat the hell did I just agree to? The weekend? With Craig. My heart is beating so fast it's going to bust out of my chest. I'd be lying if I said I never thought of this. That this isn't a dream come true in many ways. I've been drooling over Craig for years. I never thought he saw me as anything more than a friend, at best.

I finish paying at the counter and the look he gives me makes my knees weak. The girl behind the counter is practically eye-fucking him, but his eyes are on me.

"Ready, doll?" he drapes an arm around me. I can feel the envious stare from the girl at the counter burning into me— choke on your envy! He's mine, all mine... until Monday. Then, I guess we go back to being friends? I'll worry about it then. Right now, all I can think about is his hand on my back, that bag in his hand. What exactly does he have planned for us? I can't wait to find out. I may have the mother of all hangovers right now; my hands are trembling, and I cannot tell if that's a side effect from the alcohol or the thoughts of Craig on top of me again.

I'm no stranger to sex, having a long-term relationship, albeit a toxic one under my belt, and my share of short-lived romances, but last night was different. We were good together, better than good. I've never had a guy make my toes curl and my hips buck like that; my body was not my own last night. It was his and Craig knew exactly what it needed, where I needed to be touched, and how...

I panicked this morning, waking up beside him. He was just as drunk as I was last night. What if he didn't recall last night? I thought as much until he asked me about the pill. When he said he wanted more I could not believe it. Craig wants more... of me. ME!

We get back to the hotel fast enough. Standing in the

elevator I can feel his eyes roam over me. I squirm a little. As we get back to the room his phone rings. He glances at it and instantly lights up.

"Hello, Josie, my auld flower," Craig sings.

Josie— Josephine to everyone else. Craig's grandmother. She practically raised him. His mother died when he was eight and his dad couldn't handle it. Josie took Craig in and raised him. The woman is on a pedestal with him, as she should be.

Craig drops the bag on the table and walks onto the balcony to talk to his grandmother. I glance at the clock ten-past-eleven, I've still got time to shower before I've to be at the salon.

Closing the door to the bathroom, I hear Craig's booming laugh before stepping into the shower. This is just what I need. To wash away the evidence of last night, I cannot very well go to my brother's wedding stinking of stale alcohol. I grab the shampoo, creating a lather as I work it into my hair.

I feel better already, more awake, clean. The water feels good, the temperature feels good, the body pressing up against me—

"Craig?"

His hands snake around, cupping my breasts. He peppers my neck in soft, featherlight kisses that send a shiver through me.

"You smell so good," he whispers. Craig's hand slides between my legs, I gasp at the sensation.

"Craig!"

His strokes are slow, deliberate... delicious.

"Relax, doll, I got you."

Spinning me, he backs me up until my rear hits the wall, then his lips are on mine. A kiss that's desperate and full of want. A kiss that steals the air from my lungs.

The water rains down on us and my God does he look good wet. His lips fall to my neck, Craig dips a finger inside me, then another. His fingers expertly curling in me hitting just the right spot, and I feel my legs begin to shake.

* * *

She's so alluring right now. Soaking wet, moaning, trembling. I've barely touched her. She's so responsive, it's intoxicating. I reach over and turn off the shower, pulling her out with me. I can't touch her at the ceremony, in fact, the rest of the day is going to be damn near impossible to get her alone. So, I'm making sure I get my fix now.

My lips fuse with hers— I can't help it, she looks delicious. Walking her back to the bed, she falls onto the mattress, and I sink to my knees. Kissing my way up those long legs of hers, splaying them open. I take one look at that glistening entrance and any shred of willpower I had left is gone.

How is it possible for a woman to taste this sweet? Every flick of my tongue and she moans, her hands running through my hair, the sounds are turning me feral. I need more. Teasing her little bud out from under the hood, I wrap my lips around her clit and suck, pressing two fingers inside her, then three. I want to hear her scream.

* * *

What the hell is he doing to me? I have no control of my body, my hips have a mind of their own. I'm clawing at the sheets, my hair, Craig. This is too intense, I can't— can't take this. I squirm, wriggle, try to get away but he's fighting me, pinning me in place. He is relentless, "Craig!" I plead.

I can't—he's going to kill me; his tongue delves inside me, and the world falls away. Nothing exists, nothing bar Craig and whatever he is doing to me.

My legs are drawn high and trembling, I have no control. None. I feel myself hurtling towards the edge at breakneck speed.

* * *

Lottie's writhing on the bed, it's a chore keeping her restrained, but I love every minute of it. She cries out, her entire body convulsing.

I've never been so turned on in my life.

I look up at her, exhausted, panting, a boneless heap on the bed. She thinks it's over— that I'm done. Oh no, baby girl, not by a long shot. I'm just getting started. Walking to the table and opening a box of condoms, her eyes go wide, watching me slide one on.

"C- Craig... I can't..." she's still panting.

"Don't worry, Lottie. I'll take care of you..." Crawling over her, I claim that pretty mouth again. "You see how good you taste, baby."

I don't give her time to answer, I'm already at her entrance. With one thrust, I bury myself to the hilt inside her. Lottie's head tips back on a moan, and I find those perfect tits. Drawing one into my mouth, my tongue dances over the nipple, my hips snap back and forth as Lottie claws at my back, all I can think about is fucking her breathless.

She reaches up, hauling me down for a fiery kiss. Her teeth snag on my bottom lip and suddenly I'm not deep enough. Flipping Lottie on her stomach I enter her from behind.

I don't even need to ask, as soon as I'm inside her, Lottie brings her legs together, sealing me in. "Fuck, Lottie..."

* * *

A groan rumbles through Craig's large chest and I know he's close. I'm still seeing stars from the orgasm he gave me. He feels so good, so incredibly good. He leans forward nibbling on my shoulder, his moans are a perfect sensual symphony. Tugging my hips upward, I feel Craig slide a hand between my legs—he cannot be serious.

I can't take this. He's pumping inside me while teasing the ever-loving hell out of me. I can't breathe, I'm going to die. This is too much.

This is too much.

I'm tumbling towards the edge again; Craig is right there with me. His groans are more desperate, his thrusts more forceful, his body tensing.

"Fuck... Lottie, I'm close."

I barely hear him; I'm biting on the pillow muffling my own cries. A few more thrusts and he's there, roaring out his release.

He pulls out, grinning victoriously, rubbing his eyes to clear his vision. "You Goddess."

I don't have time to answer, his lips are on mine again. When he pulls away, I glance at the clock, quarter-to-twelve. *Shit!*

Craig follows my gaze and groans. "You have to go?" Is he actually pouting? I've never seen him pout before.

"Afraid so."

He leans in, kissing me again, "try not to look too gorgeous. I'll have a hard enough time keeping my hands off you as it is."

CRAIG

I'm in trouble, serious fucking trouble. What the hell is she doing to me? After Lottie left for the salon, I had the good sense to set an alarm— I passed out shortly after. I was drained. I needed to reboot. The problem is as soon as I woke up I wanted to see her. Needed to see her. Like I hadn't just spent the best part of an hour in her. I've had her twice in the space of twelve hours and it's not enough. She's like crack, one taste of her and I'm craving another hit.

I wasn't even in the room when she got back, Jay banged down the door just before two, the last hurrah before sending Nick down the aisle. I couldn't give a rat's furry ass about Nick right now. I wanted to see Lottie, to kiss her, to hold her. I've got her until Monday, she's mine until then. The fact that I must share her with everyone else today is pissing me off.

"Craig, it's so good to see you!" It's Anna, Lottie's cousin. Conceited is not the word to describe her, she thinks the sun shines out of her ass. I wouldn't get up on her to get over a wall.

"Anna, good to see you," she leans in to kiss my cheek, I allow it considering the day that's in it.

"How are you?"

"Good thanks, you?"

"Fabulous as always," she looks over my shoulder, looking for someone. "No date?"

"No."

"Strange for you."

I shrug in response. Strange for me? Like she knows me, piss off, Anna. I catch sight of Lottie's mom entering the room and excuse myself.

"There's my favourite girl."

"Craig," she outstretches her arms. "How's the head?"

"Better now," I chuckle.

"How's Nick?"

"He's good. Jay just made him neck a whisky for good luck. Help settle the nerves and all that."

"Good, good. My Lottie not around?"

"Not that I've seen," believe me I've been looking. "She was booked in for hair and makeup for twelve so— I'm assuming she should be here soon."

"Bertie being on her best behaviour, I hope?"

"Nothing out of the ordinary for her."

"I better go say hello or she'll start a war. Be sure to save me a dance later?"

"Only the best for my girl," I wink. I like Kim, always have, she's laid back. Great fun to be around at these Evans family events. Lottie looks more like Kim than Nick does, minus the blonde hair, that's probably the only thing Nick got from Kim that Lottie didn't.

I turn to scan the room again and my jaw hits the floor. Lottie, sweet, perfect, gorgeous Lottie is wearing a figure-hugging, high-slit champagne dress and I'm fairly sure there is an oyster in my pants right now. I have no words. No words to describe just how devastatingly perfect she is. How beautiful she looks. I'm staring, I know I'm staring. I can't help it. I can't look away.

She's coming straight for me.

"Craig," Nick calls.

No! Don't do this! Don't make me move. I turn to find I'm being beckoned over the other side of the room.

Great. Lottie is sitting to the left with her mother, aunts, cousins, and I'm stuck with the assholes from Nick's football club.

"Is that Nick's sister?" The jughead of the group asks.

"She's hot," the whippet nudges the jughead then looks across to another who looks like Idris Elba's ugly sister.

"I wouldn't mind having a go of her," ugly Elba states.

"Shut your fucking mouth," all heads turn to me.

"What's your problem?" the ugly sister asks; his shirt is creased— would it have killed him to pick up an iron?

"We're here for Nick's wedding. You're not in the locker room now. Cop on, and don't be disrespecting his sister."

"How's that hangover?" Jay teases.

"Piss off, Jay."

Jay sniggers and turns around, ignoring me.

The music soon starts and Abbie walks in, everyone with their oohs and aahs— don't get me wrong, she looks beautiful. Despite looking at her with the rest of the crowd when she enters, I cannot tell you one thing about her dress other than it's white. I cannot tell you one defining feature on the woman because I'm too focused on the champagne beauty opposite me.

I should be over there with her, holding her. Instead, I'm over here with these wankers going on about the footy. I don't care what team you support and why. I don't care that you got shitfaced, pissed in the wardrobe, and your Mrs went ballistic— and by the way, for the record, Pacific is an ocean! Try picking up a book you inbred asshole!

My phone vibrates.

Lottie

You ok, batman?

I look over, locking eyes with her. Why? Why is it frowned upon for me to abduct her right now?

You

Counting down the hours until I can get you out of that dress, doll ;)

This is painful— excruciating. The ceremony went on for an hour and a half! My ass is killing me. The bride and groom got whisked away for congratulatory declarations, and Lottie got swept away in the mob.

Urgh, I hate people.

"Craig."

Piss of, Bertie! "Yeah?"

"Have you met my Debbie yet?"

In other words, she's single, you're single, would you please bend the knee and give me some grand kiddos.

"No, I haven't."

Bertie calls over Debbie. One look at her and I'd rather lower myself on a cactus. "Debbie, this is Craig. He's Charlotte's roommate. He is a carpenter, owns his own business, single—"

"Actually... I'm seeing someone, Bertie."

"Oh? But you're here alone?"

"It's relatively new. Didn't want to ask Nick to change the seating plan last minute. You know yourself," I shrug and glance over her shoulder. "Ah, there's Nick now. If you'll excuse me. Debbie, lovely to meet you."

Run, Forrest Run!

"Craig, have you seen Lottie?" Nick looks about ready to crack, he must have been searching for her.

"Can't say I have, why?"

"We need her for the pictures."

"I think she said she was going to sneak a peek at the hall," Tiffy calls as she practically skips to the cocktail bar.

"I'll go get her; tell her you want her. She's most likely raiding the sweet cart."

"Great, thanks."

I catch her coming out of the hall and pounce, pulling her

through the open side door. Pinning her hands above her head, I press myself against her, our lips fusing, her tongue brushing against mine. Sweet ecstasy.

"I told you not to look so damn gorgeous," I nip at her ear, drawing out a breathy moan.

"I'm not—"

"You're stunning, Lottie." Lacing my fingers with hers, my lips brush hers again.

"Someone could see..." she blushes.

Like I give a damn. "Nick wants you for the pictures, he sent me to look for you," I step back reluctantly.

"Duty calls," she smiles warmly, brushing her hands over her dress, she steps inside and I'm in desperate need of a drink.

It's quarter-to-nine by the time the dinner is finished. I can't listen to more drivel from Nick's mates from footy, I slip outside to the smoking area. Not a sinner in sight, just me... and Lottie?

"What are you doing here?"

"Hiding from Bertie," her thumbs are dancing across the screen of her phone, most likely sending a quick text to Shannon since Tiffy is inside.

"As good of a reason as any. You look beautiful," I must have told her at least twenty times by now but it never stops being true. She sits beside me, that overwhelming urge to touch her washes over me.

"What are you wearing under that?"

"Nothing..." her eyes gleam wickedly.

"If you're winding me up..."

"Check."

Where we are in the gazebo is out of the direct line of sight of the hotel. Is it worth the risk of someone catching us? My eyes flit to Lottie, my heart starts pounding.

I slide my hand up the slit of her dress, then shove the fabric aside. No underwear. None! Not so much as a string down there. I'm already beginning to throb.

I go to move my hand further, but she moves away. Straddling me on the bench, her lips come crashing down on mine, sucking the air from my lungs.

My hands find her ass and I pull her closer, her dress bunching up. It would be so easy to take her here and now. Too easy.

Someone could see.

I don't care. I'll risk it.

When I pull back, I see the desire in her eyes, the only thing separating us is a thin layer of fabric.

"Lottie," my words come out almost breathlessly. I pull her back for another desperate kiss and feel her grinding against me, drawing out a moan.

"Lottie," I am so turned on right now, my god, if she keeps doing this I won't be able to hold out.

A burst of music booms from inside, someone is approaching from the side door. Shit!

Lottie jumps off me, fixing her dress in place. This was too close. We have to be cautious.

I glance back at her, chest heaving as she brushes her hand over her hair to compose herself. I feel myself being drawn closer. I finally have her, even if it is just temporary, I cannot keep my hands off her. How the hell am I supposed to go back in there and pretend that everything is normal when the only thing I want to do is hold her, kiss her, claim Lottie for myself.

This weekend is going to be a lot harder than I thought.

LOTTIE

*W*e have to hurry back inside when we see Nick's friends open the door to the gardens. Of course, my mom collared Craig as soon as we came back and now has him twirling her around the dance floor. He doesn't seem to mind, he does it all with a smile on his face. It's nice to see.

Michael never would have done that. He never really got on with mom, which is weird considering mom would talk the ears of a brick wall. She is just one of those fun-loving people. Always has been. She never liked Michael, that should have been the first hint for me to get out of that relationship, fast.

It's odd, I met Craig shortly after Michael and I got together. While Michael would be on the phone texting and generally keeping to himself at barbecues and birthdays, Craig would keep up with mom, dancing, joking, helping her when he could. Mom adores Craig, I doubt I'd ever have to worry about her approval with him. Nick, on the other hand— I glance over, he's spinning Abbie around on the floor, his bright smile mirroring hers, they look so happy.

I doubt Nick would approve of me and his friend. Then again, I don't need to worry about his approval. Craig and I... whatever it is we are doing; it will be over soon.

I don't want this to end. We are so good together; I know Craig must think so too. We know each other, we get on great. His kiss alone steals the breath from my lungs. I always thought that was a figure of speech until I kissed him, and the sex—it's the best of my life. Craig barely touches me and it's like every nerve ending in my body screams. The way he looks at me like he worships me... it's nice to feel wanted, desired.

Baby got back just came on and wouldn't you know, mom is up there twerking like the best of them— poor Craig.

I grab Jay, pulling him onto the dance floor. He's a great deterrent for Nick's football buddies. I want to dance with my friends, not be felt up by some middle-aged idiot that peaked in his early twenties and still thinks he's hot as shit.

Tiffy doesn't seem to mind me commandeering her man, she knows the drill as does Jason. I love Jason, he is boyishly charming, with dirty-blonde hair, and never takes himself too seriously. He and Craig have been friends for twenty-plus years, they are each other's ride or die. It's hard to think that either of them could be violent. From what Craig has told me, Jay got one too many beatdowns from his stepfather when he was young, snapped one night, and broke his nose, his arm— it sounded like the bastard deserved it.

Craig... well, after his mom died, and his dad left— it's safe to say he had some anger issues. A bit ironic that both are friends with Nick and that Jay wound up with Tiffy of all people.

* * *

She's stunning, absolutely stunning. Peeking over Kim's shoulder, I notice Lottie and Jay on the other side of the dance floor. Lottie is smiling, that gorgeous smile that reaches her eyes and makes her nose crinkle. She's happy. Truly happy, and I like to think I played a part in that today.

Addicted to love comes on and I feel like Robert Palmer is calling me out right now, this shit just got personal.

Kim's singing along to the words.

I risk another peek, Lottie's eyes lock on mine, and I'm grinning giddily like a kid that just found his father's playboys for the first time.

Jay's head snaps around, he sees me staring... *shit.* His eyes narrow and he says something to Lottie— whatever it is it makes her laugh and I can swear she's blushing.

Crap. Look away, back to Kim.

Wait you're not Kim. How the hell did I end up with the busty bridesmaid? A bra would be good, love. Under this lighting, your dress is practically see-through. I could hang cowbells off those nipples.

* * *

"So, you're really not going to admit it?" Jay presses.

"Admit what?"

"That something is going on with you, and Craig," his amber eyes sparkle, he shoots me a mischievous grin.

"There is noth—"

"Lottie, please. You have had the biggest crush on him for how long now? Four years?"

I hate Tiffy for telling him. "We're just friends."

"Yeah? So are we, and Craig never looks at me like that," Jay chuckles, twirling me outwardly then drawing me back in.

"Like what?"

"Like he's two seconds away from dry humping my leg."

I throw my head back, laughing. How am I supposed to answer that?

I spot Craig at the bar a short time later, he is ordering drinks by the truckload but for once, not for himself. He is handing out shots and double vodkas to Jay, Mom, Tiffy, Abbie, and Nick. Hell, even Bertie is getting in on the action. What is he doing?

Not surprisingly within the next hour, half the wedding party has retired to bed, everyone else hanging on by a thread. The heavyweight drinkers are the only ones left standing and not one of them seems to notice that half the guests have gone to bed.

"Time to go."

I turn to see him standing behind me, smirking.

"No one is going to notice," Craig's hands are shoved in his pockets, he turns to look over the stragglers.

"Did you deliberately get our friends drunk so you could sneak off with me, Barnes?"

"That's part of the plan."

"What's the other part?"

Craig takes my hand and leads me away from the music, away from our friends, and into the elevator. I'm half expecting him to pounce on me again, but he doesn't. He drapes an arm around me, holding me close to him until the door opens and we are on our floor.

Closing the door behind us, I am swiftly backed into the wall. He reaches down, pulling my dress over my thighs, his rough hands skim over me, sending shivers down my spine, waking every nerve in my body.

One hand comes up to my hair, grasping a handful at the nape of my neck, he angles my head to the side. Feeling his nose skim off my exposed skin, his lips trail behind my ear, down to the nape of my neck, and back up again.

"Beautiful," he leans in close and kisses me, grinding his body against mine. His tongue slips deep inside my mouth, then he pulls away. Craig smiles a heartbreakingly sexy grin that causes me to gulp.

He kisses me passionately, a kiss that makes my toes

curl. I make short work of his shirt, pulling it overhead. Barely a push from him and his pants are down, he's reaching for a condom on the table.

I lick the palm of my hand then wrap it around his length. Craig gifts me a breathy moan in response. He kisses me again, hot, messy, desperate.

Tearing the wrapping with his teeth, he rolls the condom on, his eyes never leaving mine. I'm boosted into his arms, legs wrapped around his waist. Craig rubs back and forth against my wet folds, teasing me. I let out a frustrated moan, I need to feel him in me, need to feel him that delicious stretch of him filling me. Claiming me.

I can't take it. I need him. I'm not waiting any longer. Reaching down, I guide him into me. My eyes flick to him, finding him grinning. "Can't wait, baby?"

"I've waited long enough."

His lips fuse with mine, his hips start to move. My God, he feels so good. I feel his hot breath on my neck, hear his raspy moans. He angles his hips, rubbing somewhere indescribably satisfying. My legs already beginning to tremble.

"Harder... please," I beg.

He braces one hand on the wall. Craig has officially ruined me for other men, I'm never going to recover from this. I'll never be able to be with another man.

It's not enough. My God, it's not enough. I have him inside me, I'm clawing at his back, his lips are everywhere, yet I still need more.

Craig pivots, placing me on the table, pushing my legs up and together. He slams into me, the table rattles. I doubt it can hold us, not like this, not with the force he's putting behind those hips.

* * *

The table is knocking against the wall, I stop, pick Lottie

up and bring her to the bed. I follow her to the mattress and slide back inside her. Her legs are sprawled over my shoulders. Her breath is coming in laboured pants, her lipstick smeared, and she is begging me not to stop.

Whatever my girl wants, my girl gets.

I look at her, her head tilts back, her eyes are closed, she's got this sexy little pout that she does when she's close— I need to get her there. I need to hear her cry out.

I give her everything I have. *Everything.*

Her moans grow louder, and I can feel her muscles clenching, my girl is ready.

She calls out my name, hauling me down to her.

"You're so fucking beautiful, baby." I'm lost, drowning in the sensation of her. The feel of her skin, the touch of her lips, the sound of her moaning. Devastating. That's the only word I can think of to describe her— to describe this— our lovemaking— it's fucking devastating.

I can't hold back. I'm seeing stars.

Muffling my cries in the pillow, I feel Lottie beneath me, rolling her hips, bringing me through this earth-shattering orgasm.

Turning on my back, I'm left panting, sweating, exhausted. I have never come so hard in my life.

Holding out my arms, she crawls into them, I hug her tightly and let out a content sigh. Nuzzling into her, she smells amazing, I'm still seeing stars but that does not take away from having Lottie in my arms right now.

Waking up to my phone vibrating somewhere on the floor, I crawl out of bed. Lottie's still sleeping, curled into the pillow. I count three discarded condoms slung about the room; I know the fourth is somewhere over near the nightstand.

I'm knackered. I've no idea how I'm not dead. My balls are drained.

I look at the phone, it's Jay.

"Yeah?"

"Are you going down for breakfast?"

"Are you joking?"

"Dying too?" he grumbles, still sounding half asleep.

"Yeah," I turn to see Lottie stirring. "Not got much sleep."

"I know the feeling, Tiffy spent most of the night with her head in the pot," he yawns. "How's Lottie?"

"Still asleep."

"How many shots did we do last night?"

"Enough." I made sure of that.

"I hear you, right, well I'm going to sleep this off then. No one seems to be up for it this morning. See you for dinner later then, yeah?"

"Yeah, ok." I put the phone down. This is perfect, everyone is dying with a hangover. I've Lottie to myself today. For the morning, at least.

"Who was that?" she asks groggily from the bed.

"Jay, they're all dying. Breakfast is cancelled."

"Thank God."

"Didn't want to go?"

"Can't move."

I step for the bed, brushing the hair from her face. She's exhausted but glowing.

"Breakfast in bed?" this is not right; Lottie should look like she's been dragged over a hedge backwards. She has giant panda eyes and drop-dead Fred hair, how does she still look so good?

"Please."

I dial down for room service, Lottie turns, sliding her head onto my lap. She must be sore by now. This morning is not going to be about sex for us, no. I don't think I have another round in me. Instead, we can spend the morning in bed, and I'll treat her to a hot bath before dinner. She's mine until tomorrow. I want to make sure I treat her right in the little time we have left.

LOTTIE

*I*t was still early when Jason rang us this morning about breakfast. While everyone else was nursing their raging hangovers, Craig and I were in bed. Indulging in every carb imaginable, washing it down with countless coffee and fresh fruit juices.

I love being around him, I always have. It doesn't matter what we pack away, Craig never guilts me about what I eat. He never suggests I diet or throws any shady remarks in my direction. I've always been comfortable with him. He has been my one constant for the last two years. He is beautiful, with his sparkling grey eyes and his thick brown hair. As attractive as Craig is, he is first and foremost my friend.

He pulls me on his lap, trying to be somewhat romantic with the fruit bowl, and instead knocks it all over the bed. He doesn't even get mad about it; he just laughs it off and pulls me closer.

After we eat, we lie back down. Our legs tangling to-gether. Craig traces circles on my arm with the tips of his fingers. Somewhere between talking and watching bad Sunday T.V, I fall back to sleep on his chest.

When I wake up, it is to the sound of water running. Glancing about the room, I notice Craig is nowhere in sight. He must be in the shower. I hear his phone vibrating and glance and the name. Josie.

"Hi, Josephine, how are you?"

"Charlotte? How are you? Is my Craig anywhere around?"

"He's just in the shower. I can get him to call you back if you like?"

"Oh no, that's fine. Can you just tell him that my new kitchen is coming on Wednesday?"

"Oh, very nice, upgrading again."

"These things have to be done," she laughs.

Anytime Josephine needs work done in the house, Craig will do it. Why get a team of people to fit a kitchen for her when he can do it? Why hire an electrician when Craig will give Jason a boot up the ass to get over and do it for her. It's one of the many ways he looks after the woman.

"Don't worry, I'll let him know."

"Great, you have a good day, Charlotte!"

"You, too." I hang up, grinning for no reason at all— he really is perfect.

I turn to find Craig standing behind me wrapped in a towel. "I thought I heard you."

I blush, I don't know why I answered his phone. I should have brought it into him. "Sorry," I hold out the phone for him to take. "Your nan wanted to remind you about her kitchen coming on Wednesday."

"It's the kitchen this week, watch she'll have me tiling her bathroom in a few weeks," Craig smirks. He doesn't even bother reaching for his phone or even look the slightest bit annoyed with me for answering it.

He turns into the bathroom, and I follow on instinct. Hopping up on the counter, I watch him turn off the shower then spin for me. His phone rings. Jason again.

Craig comes closer, forcing my legs open to accommodate him. Then reaches for his phone. "Yeah?"

I can hear some of Jason's muffled conversation, his words are drowned out quickly when Craig looks at me, something I can't put my finger on sparking behind his eyes.

"Mmm, hmm," tilting my chin up with his fingers, his

lips brush mine. His kiss is slow, deliberate.

"How much?" He pulls away, his attention now on the phone. It's obviously a business call. Still, he's right in front of me, practically naked, with beads of water running down his sculpted chest. That last kiss has me aching for him again.

Sliding my hands up his chest, I scoot forwards, dropping soft open-mouth pecks to his neck. He lets out a soft breathy moan. His arm snakes around me, his fingers grazing my back. Wrapping my hair around his hand, he tugs, my neck snaps back.

He's on me in an instant, nipping and sucking at my neck. "No, Wednesday's no good for me."

I slide off the counter while he's distracted, taking his hand, and leading him to the bed.

"I promised Josie, it'll have to be another day."

Pushing him back on the bed, his towel falls to the floor. Craig is propped up on his forearms, the phone in mid-air. His eyes darken to a stormy grey as I drop to my knees.

I offer him a sultry smile; he watches me with his mouth ajar. Keeping my eyes on his, I take him into my mouth, and his head tips back on a moan.

"What? No, I'm fine..." his hand brushes my hair to the side.

I tease him with slow licks from top to bottom, then let my tongue dance around the head, sucking lightly. I look up, Craig is biting on his knuckles.

I take his full length, feeling him hit the back of my throat then I hum, his hips buck in response.

"Next week is good! What? I don't know when... whenever!"

Flicking my tongue over the broad tip, I look up at him, grin then slide my lips over his shaft, licking the base with my tongue. I feel his hand on the back of my head, pulling me closer while his hips buck up.

"I gotta go— What? No— Josie's calling... yeah, bye!" Craig hangs up, the phone drops on the bed, both hands are on me in a heartbeat.

"Just like that, baby," he growls. "You're so good at that." Craig's breathing haphazardly, his hips jolting forward, I can tell he's close. Pumping him with my hand and mouth, I hollow out my cheeks and suck hard.

He writhes on the bed, sliding to his elbows then collapsing to the mattress. I love watching him, seeing how feral he gets, how he claws at his hair, the sheets— how he calls my name as he comes undone.

I kiss my way back up his body, he looks elated, serene. "I can't feel my legs," he chuckles. His arms drape around me, holding me close.

A knock comes on the door, both of our eyes widen. I jump off the bed, looking for something to throw on. Craig grabs the towel, stumbles into the wall, and runs into the bathroom.

I toss the condom boxes into my bag and scan the room for any evidence of our rigorous sexcapades. Nothing. Great, Craig cleaned up earlier.

I crack the door open to see Tiffy standing on the other side looking like she has been hit by a freight train.

"Please tell me you have some painkillers spare," she moans.

"Yeah, of course."

She follows me into the room, her nose crinkling. "It smells like sizzled ass in here."

"The heating was cranked up last night and Craig is still leaking whisky from his pores, what do you expect?"

"Where is he?"

"The shower, possibly dead. He's been in there for

ages," I pull out a sleeve of ibuprofen and hand it over.

"You're a godsend." Tiffy's hands tremble as she tears the foil to get to the tablets.

"You should head back to bed. You look like you need the rest."

"I might just do that, thank you!"

"Welcome," I crack the door open, allowing her to pass me. "Dinner is at seven, yeah?"

"Yeah. Nick is down in the pool with Abbie and a few of the boys from his football club if you want to head down?"

"I'll pass," I scrunch up my nose, the thought alone makes me want to stick my head in the toilet.

"Can't say I blame you."

As soon as I close the door, Craig comes out from hiding. "Do you think she heard us?"

"She would have said."

He leans down, kissing me. "You know, I was planning on a sex-free day today," he mutters as he nibbles my ear.

"Sick of me already, Barnes?"

"Not even close."

My phone pings, a message from mom.

A picture of her half-dead in the bed, makeup still on from last night.

Mom

Feeling Fresh this morning. What about you?

You

Never better

I snap a quick selfie with Craig— a close-up so I'm not giving mom a free show— although knowing her, I doubt she would complain.

Mom texts back immediately.

Mom

Assholes

You

Love you too xx

We get dressed and head outside, walking into town; it takes about twenty minutes. We go for a coffee, then browse some of the stores. Picking up a small haul in the local bookshop then Craig treats me to lunch. The entire time we are together, he holds me close, our fingers laced. He pulls me in for a kiss every so often and I melt every time.

Why do we have to end things tomorrow? Why did we put a stupid timeline on this? Do I tell him I want more? That I want to continue this, whatever this is? Does he want the same? Or does he just want exactly what he proposed, a weekend to "get it out of our systems," and then go back to normal? But I can't go back, I know I can't. It has barely been two days of us— of this, and I already know that I'm falling hard for him.

CRAIG

I've never dreaded going home as much in my life.

Yesterday was amazing, I had Lottie to myself until four. I took her out, could kiss her and hold her as much as I wanted because no one we knew was around. Everyone was back at the hotel.

Of course, we brought Kim back something from the bakery to help entice her out of bed and to get ready for dinner, like Lottie, her mom can't resist anything sweet. Then I had Lottie back behind closed doors, I got to treat her, made her up a bath because my girl was still feeling the effects of the last few days. I rubbed her raw, I couldn't help it. I couldn't keep my hands off her, but I could make her feel better. I picked up some bath fizzer thing because you know girls like that stuff. Little did I know it turned into a disco ball when dropped in the water, glitter everywhere! Thank God I didn't have to clean that one up.

She deserves to be treated. Taken care of. I've seen the last few assholes she dated, it's no wonder they were sent packing pretty quickly, and don't even get me started on Michael! That asshat never deserved her; she doesn't like to talk about it, but I know enough. I saw the way he'd treat her at birthdays and other Evans family events. Constantly making snide comments about the way she looked, or her weight and passing it off as a joke. Then he went and cheated on her and had the brass balls to tell her it was her fault for 'letting herself go.'

Dinner was interesting, to say the least. We were one of the first there and picked the seats in the corner, facing one another. Playing footsie under the table like a pair of love-struck teenagers.

When we got back to the room, we were both beat, depleted from the weekend fuckfest. Lottie slipped on one of my shirts and fell asleep watching family guy. I don't want the shirt back; it looks better on her.

This morning I woke to her nuzzling into me, her hands rubbing me awake and I could not believe my luck. Waking up with that gorgeous woman practically mounting me. The way she can move her body, roll her hips it's fucking incredible. I had to have her again before check-out.

Now I'm sitting in the car with Jay and Tiffy for the next three hours. Lottie is only inches from me and I can't touch her. I hate this. We said Monday and it's finally here. We left the hotel and essentially any romantic feelings behind when we checked out. That was the plan—stupid fucking plan.

"Please, have you not heard him?" Tiffy's voice pulls me back to reality.

"Are you going to take that?" Lottie turns to me, laughing.

"Come on, Craig, you don't strike me as the type. Your version of foreplay is probably saying bite the pillow, I'm going in dry."

Jay snorts—asshole!

"Is Jay letting you down that much that you have to think about me?"

"I'm more than satisfied, thank you."

Jay turns to wink at Tiffy in response. Lottie's phone rings, I glance at her, her brow furrowing, debating if she should answer or not.

"Hello?" she looks to Tiffy then back at the phone. "Hello?" she hangs up and puts the phone away. Noticing me staring, she shrugs "wrong number."

"So, what's the plan?" Jay asks as he pulls off at the

services.

"I don't know about you lot, but I'm fit for bed!" Tiffy yawns then goes in search of red bull.

"Lottie?" Jay asks.

"Yeah, I need a sugar buzz, I'm dying."

Jay drops us home, there is an initial awkwardness when he leaves and it's just me and Lottie. We shuffle our asses upstairs and unpack, it takes about half an hour before I run into her again in the kitchen.

"Take out?" she suggests, holding up two menus.

"Pizza?"

"Good choice," she smiles, placing the menus down. Then rings in our order, she doesn't need to ask, we get the same thing every time. A large meat feast pizza with BBQ base, garlic bread, and cookies.

"Be about half an hour," she places the phone down then looks at me. I really want to kiss her. "So... what now?"

"What to do or with us?"

"Both... I guess. We did say Monday."

"Technically it's still Monday for a few more hours."

Her eyes sparkle back at me, that wicked smirk stretching across her face. "What are you suggesting?"

"Well," I tug her closer by the hips. "We could spend the evening in bed."

"My bed or yours?" she slides her hands around my neck, fingers tangling in my hair.

"Both?"

"How do you plan on doing that?"

"We can bring the food upstairs and throw on Netflix," my lips find the spot just below her ear.

"Uh-huh, that's one bed."

"Then I can drag you into my bed and fuck you until

the headboard snaps."

To say we indulge is a gross understatement. I eat the majority of the pizza while Lottie makes quick work of the cookies. We turn on Beetlejuice— watch none of it. I spend most of the film with my tongue in her mouth.

I take her in her bed, up against the wall, the landing, my room—the second floor of our house looks like someone broke in, there are clothes and turned over furniture everywhere. I make good on my threat of fucking her until the headboard snaps, only it's the slats underneath that give way—looks like we have to share a bed again until I get around to fixing that... oops.

She's lying in my arms, in that crumpled-up pile I called a bed and I know I'm not going to be able to walk away from this, from her. I can't just go back to the way things were, allow another man to touch her. The thought alone has my blood boiling. She's mine. I don't know how I got her, but there is no way I'm letting her go. To hell with Nick. He will just have to accept it. I've stayed away long enough, four years to be exact. I'm done.

I drop my lips to her arm and trail up to her neck, she lets out a soft moan and I know she's still awake, "Lottie?"

"Hmm?"

"What if we maybe... don't put a timeline on this?"

No response. Shit. Did I read this all wrong?

"What?" she turns to me, her eyes warm but she looks, I don't know... happy? Confused? Both?

"I mean if you want to... that is... maybe we could... possibly... see where this is going?"

"What about Nick?"

"He's not joining us," did I just say that? *What the fuck is wrong with you?* Thank God she's laughing and not jumping out the window. "He's away for the next two weeks, right?"

"Yeah," she curls in closer, snaking her arms around me, playing with the tufts of hair at the back of my neck.

"That gives us some time to figure this out..." *So much for not putting a timeline on it, genius!* "It was only a thought. If you don't want to—"

She hauls me down to her, her tongue sliding across the seam of my lips, and I am only too happy to grant her access.

My phone rings. I ignore it, letting it ring out.

It rings again.

"Shouldn't you get that?" Lottie laughs.

"It's probably just Jay," I roll her onto her back, pinning her hands above her head.

The phone rings again.

"Someone better be fucking dying!" I scramble over what remains of my bed to get out of the room and into Lottie's to find that damn phone.

"Josie?"

"Did I wake you?"

"No, I was in the shower."

"Can you bring me out to Ikea tomorrow, my car is not big enough."

"Planning on running out with half the shop?"

"You don't mind, do you?"

"No, no." I spot Lottie strutting back to her room, putting more emphasis on her hips than usual—the little minx. "I need a new bed anyway. I'll pick you up about lunchtime?"

"Good, see you then!"

Bless the woman for not asking questions.

I dropped Lottie off at Kim's on my way to Josie's, they're going off for a spa day to detox after the wedding, considering the amount of alcohol Kim put away over the weekend, a detox is probably not a bad idea.

I didn't even get a chance to get out of the van when I pulled up at Josie's, she was already at the door making a beeline for me with that handbag—the one that can rival Mary Poppins, slung around her shoulder. Any time she comes out with that, I know I have a day of it.

"How was the wedding?" she asks as we pull onto the road.

"As good as any other," I lie. Best weekend of my life, but I'm not getting into the nitty-gritty with her.

"Did you meet anyone?"

"No one of interest."

"Lottie was there..."

"Well yeah, it was Nick's wedding, I'd be a bit worried if she didn't show up." I slow us down for a red light and catch Josie giving me the side-eye. "What?"

"I like her."

You and me both.

"She's a nice girl," she continues.

"Yeah, she is."

"Attractive too."

You can say that again.

"What are you getting at, Josie?"

"You shared a room?"

Oh, no, don't go there, Josie.

"Yeah, a mix-up at the hotel," I shrug. The light turns green, and I pull off, trying not to give anything away. "No big deal, I mean, we share a house. Not much difference."

"You shared a bed, too?"

Kill me, kill me now.

"If you can call it that. Got back legless and passed out."

"You had relations..."

I almost crash the fucking van. Josie's grinning like she has a hanger stuck in her mouth.

"What? No!"

"Say that to me without the smile on your face."

"We didn't... nothing—shut up!"

"There is nothing to be ashamed about, sex is a natural thing."

"Stop. For the love of God please, stop."

"I remember your grandad and I—"

"AHHHH LALALALALALALALALA... can't hear you..."

"I hope you were safe."

The holy mortifying shame of this conversation.

We spend the guts of three hours in Ikea, my van is buckling under the pressure. I could have just fixed the bed back in the house, but I want something new. A bed where the only memories I'll have are of Lottie beneath me.

I treat Josie to lunch after— steak on a stone, can't bring the woman to McDonald's and call it a day, she raised me better than that. Imagine me bringing the woman to a drive-through, Bobby would not only roll over in his grave, but he'd also come back and haunt me for it.

My phone vibrates, I reach over to check. A picture from Lottie of her at the spa, wearing nothing but a skimpy white bikini.

When I glance up, Josie is staring at me, grinning. I hide the phone out of instinct.

"Something important?" she presses.

"Just Jay."

She cocks an eyebrow at me, still grinning.

"What?"

"Nothing."

* * *

This is nice, mom and I got facials and spent most of the day in the jacuzzi. I couldn't help but send Craig a cheeky picture of me in the bikini before I got dressed. No response though, he must be busy with Josie.

Mom and I went to our favourite Chinese restaurant after the spa, washing the food down with copious amounts of wine. White for me, red for mom.

My phone rings, the private number again. I answer but all I can hear is breathing for a second and the phone hangs up. Strange, the same thing happened yesterday.

Probably just a prank call.

"One down, one to go," Mom announces.

"You'll be waiting a long time on me," I giggle into my glass.

"No one at the wedding strikes your fancy?"

I wouldn't go that far...

"None of Nick's footballer friends?" she presses.

"As if."

"You're very picky lately," mom teases.

"Can you blame me?"

"No. Not after— so who is Craig's new girlfriend?" She asks, changing the subject.

"What?" I almost choke on my wine.

"Bertie said he told her he is seeing someone new. He never mentioned her to me."

Did he say that? My heart races, was he referring to me? No, no calm down Lottie.

"He probably just said that to get her off his back," I shrug.

"I thought as much," mom pulls out her card to pay, "my treat."

"You sure?"

"Absolutely."

We get a taxi back to Mom's and Craig swings by around seven to pick me up. Of course, it is not a quick fly-by, mom would never allow it. She parks him in the kitchen, puts on the kettle and as soon as the biscuits come out, we both know he is trapped for at least an hour.

Mom talks the ears off him about everything and

nothing, she asks him about work, Josie, the next thing I know she has him roped into doing her floors and decking for her. I don't know when he is going to get the time to do that, when Craig is at work he is usually gone by eight in the morning and often not back until after six, sometimes I don't even see him. It's not unusual for him to be gone for ten and twelve-hour shifts. When he does get back, he normally grabs something quick to eat and falls into bed.

Finally, mom permits us to leave and waves us off at the door.

"How's Josie?" I ask as soon as we get in the van.

"As inappropriate as ever," Craig says, looking in the mirrors as he steers into a three-point turn.

"Oh? What was she saying now?"

"You don't want to know."

My phone rings again.

"What's wrong?"

"This number keeps calling me. When I answer they just breathe down the phone and hang up."

Craig looks concerned, he takes the phone from me to answer. "Hello, pervert!" he grins, handing the phone back to me. "I guess they weren't too fond of that."

"I can't imagine why," I slide my hand onto his leg, Craig laces his fingers through mine and squeezes.

"You're back at work tomorrow?"

"Don't remind me."

"I'll drop you off, I've to fit Josie's kitchen for her anyway."

We stop at a red light, and I hear something slide, followed by a loud thump from the back of the van.

"What was that?"

"Our new bed."

* * *

I dragged the new bed frame and mattress into the house, dumping them by the stairs. I can't be arsed putting it together tonight, I'll do it tomorrow.

Lottie runs around getting her uniform and lunch ready for tomorrow morning, while I call Dylan and tell him to get his ass to Josie's house tomorrow. I can sort out most of the kitchen, but I'll need his help with the sink and other pipework.

I can't believe Josie today, actually asking me that stuff. Then again, I shouldn't be surprised. That woman is still living in the sixties. You know she once had the brass balls to ask me what anal beads are, yeah... most people have cute nans that make cakes and buy them ugly Christmas jumpers. Mine will sit down and have a full-on discussion about sex toys and the importance of being a generous lover.

I still cringe thinking about the birds and the bees talk she gave me when I was twelve. Didn't need the image of Bobby coming up on her like a startled donkey in my mind. That shit is the thing of nightmares.

Lottie did what she always does when she gets in in the evenings and changes straight into her pyjamas. I don't know how the woman makes an Oodie look sexy, but she does it. I never thought an oversized jumper would look so good on someone until I saw her running around the house in it.

I'm then forced to watch Moana for the millionth time, and yes, in case you are wondering I know all the words to you're welcome. Well, forced may be a bit harsh of a saying. She wanted to watch Moana and I'm happy to just hold her and endure.

By the end of the film, she's asleep on my chest. I get a text from some girl I barely remember, asking if we're still on for tomorrow night... awkward. Somehow, I doubt the 'me no speak English' excuse is going to fly here. I debate ignoring it, but then again, I don't want to be a total ass-hole. That and I don't want to risk her calling and Lottie thinking that I've someone on the side.

I type out a quick rejection, saying I got back with my girlfriend, then pause. The word jumping out at me. Girlfriend. Is that what Lottie is? Hmm... I don't think I've used that term since I was eighteen. Are we too old to use those terms now? I mean, come on I'm thirty-two, boyfriend seems a bit, I don't know... young? I make myself sound like a fossil. Manfriend— great now I sound like a dog. I'm thinking too much into this again.

* * *

I wake up having a mini-heart attack when Craig's alarm goes off. Most people use the generic sounds on their phone— at least I do! Not Craig, no, Shinedown, fly from the inside wakes me up at six in the morning!

I jump, headbutt him in the chin, the back of my head is throbbing. Great start to the morning this is. To make matters worse I stub my toe on the way to the bathroom. Holy mother of all things unholy that hurt like hell. I'm already done with the day. I want to go back to bed.

I look back to the bed, Craig is pitching a tent under the covers, still rubbing his face from where I slammed into him. "Come back to bed."

"I can't, I've work."

"So."

"So not all of us have the luxury of being our own boss, I can't be late."

"You're no fun."

I scowl at him. Do not test me without my coffee, Barnes. I will end you.

"You're sexy when you're angry."

I ignore him. Stomping my way downstairs in search of caffeine and a possible defibrillator. I bang on the kettle, it's back to reality today. I hate it. I wish I could be like Craig and work for myself. Or be like one of those influencers that make money just by sticking up a few selfies online. Urgh, life's not fair.

I turn to see him coming downstairs. Ok, life does have its upsides. Craig wraps me in his arms, squeezing me tightly, then picks me up and puts me on the counter like I weigh nothing.

Framing my face in his hands, he leans down, kissing me tenderly. Then proceeds to pour two generous mugs of coffee and offers to cook breakfast. My hero.

While I run around the house making sure I have everything for work, Craig taps away on his phone looking as relaxed as ever. When I'm ready to go he locks the door and drives me to work.

I like my job for the most part. I come in and get started on the delivery, putting the medicines on the shelves while Shannon knocks out the prescriptions. About an hour in, she gasps, I turn to see what the fuss is about, and a guy is coming into the store with two dozen, long stem red roses.

"Whose birthday is it?" I ask, knowing the girls tend to have flowers delivered from their other halves on their birthdays and special occasions.

"Charlotte Evans?" The delivery driver asks.

"Me?"

Shannon runs over immediately, bringing the flowers to me. There is a note on the side.

You make my knob throb.

xxxx

"Who is that from?" Shannon squeals.

I blush to my roots. This is so sweet and mortifying all at once. I'll kill him.

"Lottie? You've been holding out on us, spill!"

Should I say? I mean, we did agree to see where things are going. "It's from—" a couple at the counter catches my

Screw it!

attention. The guy turns and my heart sinks, "Michael?"

LOTTIE

"Michael?"

"Char?"

I cringe, he is the only one to ever call me that. I hate to admit it, but he looks good, beautiful olive skin that reminds me of Tiffy. Slicked back dark hair, clean-shaven.

Shannon proceeds to speak with the woman he is with, offering her advice on medications. I'm stood here frozen to the grey carpet of the pharmacy. My feet are starting to sweat, as are my hands— which are still clutching the roses Craig sent me.

"New service?" He nods to the roses.

"Huh?" I glance at the flowers. "Oh these, no, these are mine," my god why must I stumble over my words when he's nearby? I thought I would be past this by now.

"New man in your life?"

"Yes. There is as a matter of fact." I see Shannon give me the side-eye. I pull my rolled shoulders back in an attempt to look confident.

"Anyone I know?"

"I don't see how my love life is any of your concern."

"Wow, it was a simple question. You don't need to be like such a bitch about it," Michael crosses his arms, scowling at me. Some things, like that snarky tone of his, never change. I flinch at the sudden outburst of anger. Taking a deep breath in, my gaze is brought back to the roses. To Craig.

"A bitch?" I scoff, remembering Craig's comeback to the last time someone called me that. A Babe In Total Control of Herself. "No. I'm not doing this. Shannon, I'm putting these in the back."

"Take your time," she keeps her tone neutral as I type in the code to get to the back of the store.

How dare he come in here and start this shit! Make me feel like I did something wrong. What does it matter if he knows who it is I'm seeing? It doesn't! So why does he have to know?

Creeping to the door I peek out, watching him and the poor unfortunate with him leave. *Good riddance!*

I shoot a text over to Tiffy, letting her know what has happened. Urgh, I can't stand him! I glance at the roses and decide I better shoot Craig a text to say thank you.

> **You**
>
> Thank you for the roses, they're beautiful. You're note was horribly inappropriate though! I'll have to explain myself to Shannon xxx
>
> **Craig**
>
> But I bet it put a smile on your face ;)

It did. It really did. He knew I was dreading coming back to work and he knew how to make me feel better about it. I love that about him. I miss him already.

> **You**
>
> You are definitely Josie's grandson! xxx
>
> **Craig**
>
> I'll take that as a compliment. I'll collect you after work today xx

I almost type I love you and quickly think against it. *Jeez, am I there already? Am I in love with Craig? I think so...* even still, I don't want the first time I say it to be over text.

> **You**
>
> Please do. xxx

> **Craig**
>
> Everything ok baby? xxx

Yeah, just my ex showed up in-store today— I better not tell him, not until I see him. He'll only worry.

> **You**
>
> Yeah, I'd just rather be at home with you xxx

> **Craig**
>
> Me too baby xxx

* * *

Well, that was easy. Dylan brought Jay, Jay brought Stephen and the entire kitchen was done in four hours. The only problem is, I have another four and a half hours spare before I have to pick up Lottie from work.

She sounded a little off when she text. Maybe it's just going back to work after being away for a few days, or one of the junkies could have kicked up stink about their methadone again. Either way, I feel like I need to do something for her.

Driving into town, I end up in the Disney store. The choice is unreal— holy fuckballs, so many plush toys and that's only at the entrance. I pick her up a Stitch plushie and a Moana mug and get out of there before people start looking at me weird for being a grown man in a Disney store with no kid present.

I pass by Ann Summers and figure; lingerie is always good, right? There are some outfits in there that I would love to see Lottie in. The only problem when I get there is

I don't know what size to get her. When the girl came over to help, apparently responding "about two handfuls" is the wrong answer to give when being asked about a cup size.

I chance my arm at some of the other items and I think I'm in luck until I look at the tags. Lottie is a 12-14, I know that much, but the tags 10-12 and 14-16, they don't come in the "in-between" sizes, so do I go with the 10-12 and risk it not fitting or go with the 14-16 and risk accidentally calling her a cow? *Shit! Retreat, retreat.*

Lush... lush is good. Bath fizzer things and makeup, that's a safe bet right? Or am I telling her that she needs a bath? Fucking cum guzzling, cock sucker! This shit is hard.

By three o'clock I'm sitting in my van, staring at the accumulation of bags across from me and wondering how I managed to panic buy over five hundred quid's worth of stuff.

What do I do? Do I return it? Do I give it all to her at once, or is she going to think I'm some desperate asshole that's going to be hiding in the bushes if she rejects me? I could give some of it to Josie. Keep some of it up? I have five different perfumes from Boots because I hadn't a fucking clue what she liked. One hundred and eight quid for Givenchy, she better like it.

My phone rings and surprise surprise it's Jay. "Yeah?"

"Are you picking Lottie up from work today?"

"Yeah, why?"

"Did you know Michael showed up at her job?"

"He what?"

I hate that prick, I really do. He looks like a malnourished Jason Momoa, with none of the fucking charm. He makes up for it by coming with an extra side of sleaze. What Lottie ever saw in him I'll never know.

"Yeah. I know, Tiffy just told me."

"She never said. I knew something was up with her, I just thought— urgh, that asshole!"

"You don't think he's going to cause any shit, do you?"

"He better not."

"What if he's there when you go to pick her up?"

"I'll hit him with the van!" I'm not kidding.

"You think she'll be alright?"

"Lottie has nothing to worry about. I'll swing by her job now, wait until she's done."

"I'll keep the phone on loud just in case," Jay mutters.

"Yeah, bring bail money."

Pulling up outside the shop an hour early, scanning the streets before I get out, looking for the little weasel lurking about. I can't spot him anywhere.

Good, he better be gone.

A bit convenient that he shows up as soon as Nick is out of the country. That's fine though, if he tries anything with my girl, he'll be swallowing his teeth like painkillers.

I spot Lottie leaning over the shelves, scan the area again, then move into Costa next door before I show up with offerings for Shannon. I'll most likely get the ears talked off me by Shannon, and Katie the pharmacist. If I sweet talk them enough they might not kick me out for loitering.

Lottie is hunkered down cleaning up one of the bottom shelves. She doesn't notice me behind her.

"Hey, sexy lady."

She shoots up to her full height, those beautiful eyes sparkling back at me. "You're early?"

"Couldn't stay away."

"You!" Shannon calls, pointing directly at me.

"You told her then?"

"Is that a problem?"

"Not at all," my fingers brush hers as I walk to the counter. "Coffee?"

The words barely pass my lips when Katie runs out from the back, armed with a phone to her ear. She takes one of the cups and shoots me a thumbs up before stalking back inside. Shannon takes the offering, her eyes fixed on me the entire time like she is debating what to say.

"How's the knob?"

"Shannon!" Lottie squeals.

"Still there, thanks for asking."

Katie pops her head back out, waving for Lottie to go. "Are you sure?"

"Yeah, it's fine," she mouths.

"The place is dead anyway," Shannon shrugs.

"Ok, thanks," Lottie hurries in the back, coming out a few minutes later with her handbag, flowers, and jacket.

"Ready, baby?" I take her hand, lacing our fingers together and she nods.

"Don't be silly, wrap your willy!"

"Shannon!" Lottie growls.

We get into the van, Lottie looks nervous. "Michael was in today..."

"I know."

"You do?"

"Tiffy told Jay."

"I'm sorry..."

"Hey," I lean over, tilting her head up to look at me. "You did nothing wrong. Don't worry about it, ok?"

She nods her head, tears threatening to escape those beautiful eyes.

"Did he say anything to you?"

"No, well... he called me a bitch," she's fiddling with her hands, looking everywhere but directly at me.

"What!"

"He came in when the roses were delivered. Wanted to know who sent them and got mad when I wouldn't tell him."

"Did he now?"

"Craig..."

"No, don't apologise. Now, we are going to get you home. You are going to get into a bath while I cook

dinner tonight and then we can relax, take it easy, ok?"
Her lips are on mine. Her kiss is warm, passionate. She
kisses me like I'm her last salvation. "I love you."

I blink, dumbfounded. Did she just say that? Did I hear
her right? She loves me. Lottie loves me? Me?

*Oh, my God, will you fucking say something back, you
idiot!* "I—" *She loves me! I can't believe this; she actually
fucking loves me!* "I love you, too."

CRAIG

*L*ottie got home and jumped in the bath. Once I had everything prepped and banged in the oven, I hauled the bed upstairs and put it together then came back down and wrestled with the mattress. By the time I hit the landing I was knackered. You'd swear I ran a marathon, *why did I choose to pick up the Super King bed again?*

I hear the water sloshing about in the bathroom and peek in, catching Lottie's reflection in the mirror. *Ah, that's why.* I linger, watching her for a minute while I catch my breath. She runs the sponge over her legs, and I'm tempted to dump the mattress here and join her.

New bed, new sheets, new pillows, new girlfriend— Lottie's mine, my girl, how the hell did I manage to pull that one off? I can't believe my luck.

I set up our new bed, yes, *our bed.* She is not going back into that other room. I'll get the sledgehammer to that other bed and make sure of that. That is no longer her room or her bed. Her job is to stay on this bed that takes up half of our bloody room, and look pretty. Not that that second part is ever a hard thing for her to do, Lottie is gorgeous— naturally gorgeous. She could wear a bin bag and still be the most beautiful woman in any room.

We have dinner—nothing like a pasta bake to lift your spirits, then she goes into our room and discovers the small haul I panic bought earlier today. Lottie squeals and hides her face in her hands as she turns crimson. It was worth every cent to see her light up like that. I'd spend it again in a heartbeat.

She looks up at me through lowered lashes and I take the bait. Hauling me down for a kiss, we stumble and fall onto the bed, I quickly clear off the perfume bottles and

Moana mug— pretty much anything breakable has to be moved ASAP.

* * *

Waking up to Craig's alarm going off at 5.30 am, I groan and curl into him. He switches it off and stays with me for a little while longer before he reluctantly gets out of bed, grumbling as he searches for his pants.

"I was comfy," I pout, curling into the pillow he just came from. It smells just like him.

"Don't give me that look," he warns, jumping into his trousers. "You know I can't resist that look." Craig crawls over the bed, brushes the hair from my face, and kisses me. "I'll see you later tonight, I love you." He kisses me again.

"I love you, too."

* * *

I don't believe this, I got pulled in on my way to work. Where do you think you're going, son? Eh, I don't know, given the van the hi-vis vest, and the pissed-off look on my face that says I'd rather be in bed with my girlfriend right now than going on-site to see a bunch of ass cracks on show. I'm going to venture a guess and say work.

I'm normally quite good in the morning, I would by no means say I'm a morning person as in chipper and ready for a singsong but compared to Lottie I'm a Saint. She'd skull fuck you with a butcher's knife if you say boo to her before her coffee kicks in.

God, I love that woman.

The day is typical, nothing out of the ordinary so to speak. Jay blasts everything from the Bee Gees to Nicki Minaj, he gets at least six texts and three calls from Tiffy throughout the day and tries not to blow any of us up while rewiring the kitchen.

Dylan tells a story about his fictional sex life, really going into detail with it, too. Someone was obviously watching a lot of porn over the weekend, in between playing fortnight. We all know half of the callouses on his hands aren't from working on-site.

Stephen the nosey bastard put me in hot water when my phone went off and he looked at the text from Lottie. Nothing too incriminating as such, no sexting— thank God. I wouldn't want him thinking of her in that light. I'd be forced to bury him under the extension. He did, however, catch that it was more than just a text one would send to a roommate and of course, Jay was on my ass in a heartbeat.

"I knew it! I knew something was going on with you two!"

"And what? You want a medal?"

"Does Nick know?"

"No. And I'd appreciate it if you don't open your mouth until we tell him after he gets back."

"How long have you been sleeping with her?"

"It's not like that!"

"Oh, I know you're not just banging her. You've been drooling over her for years."

"The wedding," I admit, seeing that he isn't about to let up without answers.

"I knew it! The room smelled like a brothel. Tiffy just thought you had a vicious wan—"

"For fuck's sake," I walk away. Not arsed listening to Jay ramble on.

I check the time, 6.30 pm, "right, we're done for the day, yeah?"

"Yeah," Jay calls back.

We wrap up and I grab my tools, walking back to the van. "I don't fucking believe this."

"What?" Jay asks from the back of his car.

"Some wanker slashed my tires." There was a gang of

teenagers hanging about earlier, must have been one of them. *Shitheads.*

I pull out the phone to call the AA. I'll need to get this towed. Great, just fucking great.

You

Going to be late home tonight. Some arsehole killed my tires. Waiting for a tow xxx

Lottie

Are you serious? xx

You

As a heart attack. xxx

Lottie

Wankbags! >:(How are you going to get home? xx

You

I'll get Jay to give me a lift after I get the van towed to Mick's garage xxx

Lottie

Ok be safe. Love you xxx

You

Love you too baby girl xxx

"Are you fucking serious!"

"What now?" Jay asks, glancing in the back of the van.

"My chop saw is gone!" There goes thirteen hundred quid pissed down the drain! I hope someone sends them a boiled shite for Christmas!

"It couldn't have been those kids then, they walked right by me when I went to ring Tiffy earlier. I would have seen them with it."

"If I find out who did it, I'll kneecap the bastard!"

"Tires slashed; van robbed... who did you piss off?" Dylan asks.

"Your Ma!"

"That's uncalled for!"

"Go home, Dylan, before he stabs you," Jay advises. We load up the rest of my tools into Jay's car, no way I'm trusting the guy towing this to not fleece me.

"What now?" Jay leans against the bonnet of his car.

"We wait."

"So, Charles must have been doing some digging," Jay sighs, pulling out a smoke then tilting the box in my direction, offering me one.

"As in?" Tiffy's father is a bit on the protective side.

"We were at dinner the other day and while Tiffy was helping Sandra tidy up, Charles just comes out with "so you have been in trouble with the law in the past," he would have to dig for that shit right? I mean our records were expunged."

"What did you say?"

"I asked him to define trouble."

"And?"

"He didn't push it," Jay shrugs and lights up.

"Tiffy knows though, right? You told her?"

"Yeah, she knows. She doesn't care... it doesn't bother her or anything."

"Her dad is probably just being cautious. I mean, if you had a daughter and found out her boyfriend was locked up you'd want to know why wouldn't you?"

"Yeah, I guess..." Jay takes a long drag from his smoke, looking out in the distance.

"I wouldn't worry. I mean, it's not like you were a drug runner or sex offender or anything."

"True, just caught me off guard," he takes another drag, slowly exhaling clouds of smoke before turning to me, "Lottie knows about you, right?"

"Yeah, she's known for years. Much like Tiffy, it doesn't bother her. Funny enough, I think it's because of it that she chose to move in in the first place."

"Because she knows you can fight?"

"I don't scare easy. If Michael showed up starting any shit—"

"You'd knock the bollocks off him," Jay chuckles.

"These better not take long about getting here, I'm starving!"

LOTTIE

*B*y the time Craig got in last night, he was exhausted. He was left waiting around for over an hour on a tow, got the van brought to his friend Mick's garage, and had Jay drop him home. It was closer to nine by the time I locked eyes on him. He got in, had dinner, a shower, then passed out as soon as his head hit the pillow.

It's strange that out of all the cars parked up, they only targeted Craig's van. Then again, I don't understand half of the teenagers today— dragged up little toerags.

I had another weird breathy call earlier; you would think whoever is doing it would get bored, right? I blocked the number and went on my way.

I told mom, about Craig and me. She seemed— happy is not the word to use, ecstatic would be more appropriate. Of course, I was bombarded with questions soon after.

Nick should really let mom into the interrogation room in the future, she doesn't let up. Mom promised not to say anything to Nick until we can speak with him first, then invited us around for dinner. I had to reject that offer seeing as I'm working until seven and Craig is probably going to be in foul form after what happened. I can't say I blame him.

He had to get a taxi to Mick's garage this morning, then drive to work from there. I saw him for all of five minutes before he left, despite being a little grizzly he kissed me goodbye and told me he loved me.

I want to do something for him, but what?

I don't make the money he does; I wish I did. I'd love to be able to go out and splurge on him, but after Nick's wedding, I'm skint until payday.

I hear my phone chime from my bedside table, Craig's name flashes on the screen. Hopefully, he got sorted.

"Hello?"

"Hey, baby. Just making sure you're up for work."

"Yeah, I'm up. Did you get it all sorted?"

"Hmm? Yeah, all good now. My card's going to blow up if I keep using it."

"Well then stop spoiling me."

"I like spoiling you," I can hear him smiling, he sounds in better form than when he left this morning.

"Mom wants us over for dinner this week, she wanted us tonight actually, but I told her I'd have to check and see when you're free."

"Dinner... eh, this week?"

"Preferably, but if you can't don't worry about it. I know you're busy."

"Nah, just let me think... what day are we?"

"Friday."

"Oh yeah," I can hear Jason and Dylan in the background and I'm assuming Craig is smoking judging by the impromptu silences.

"You're not awake yet, are you?"

"Not in the slightest. Eh, I'm free tomorrow if that works? Can't do Sunday, we have to go to Josie's."

"We?"

"I didn't tell you did I?"

"No, batman, you left that part out."

"Shit, sorry."

"No, it's fine. I like Josie. She's not going to go all hippie on us and start talking about the Kama sutra, is she?"

"I fucking hope not."

"Ok, I better go get my bus. I'll cook tonight, anything you fancy?"

"You."

"Behave."

"Call me if that prick shows up again," I can tell by his tone of voice that this is not a request.

"I will. I gotta go, love you."

"Love you, too."

Another day another... whatever, I'm bored. The place is dead. The only people coming in are girls looking for last-minute tan and makeup before heading out tonight and those smart enough to stockpile for their hangovers tomorrow.

The shop is clean, all orders have been done, which means Katie, Shannon, and I can just sit around and talk about nothing. We went from discussing Nick's wedding and the whole Craig and me thing, I don't know how it happened, but we went from that to The Witcher to talking about a possible zombie apocalypse. I'd be one of the first deaths, I can't run for shit.

"So, what happened with that Michael guy?" Katie asks. She was not around when we were together, must have got curious when Shannon start cursing him out.

"He is a raging asshole!" Shannon declares with great enthusiasm.

"Well, said," I cast my eyes at the door, no customers. "He was... toxic, controlling. He would accuse me of cheating on him all the time, look through my phone, criticise my appearance, that sort of thing. In the end, he was the one that cheated on me and I finally saw him for what he was and left."

"Yeah, Shannon's right, he sounds like an asshole," Katie takes a sip of tea from the mug she has been cradling in her hands.

"Supersize that!" Shannon scoffs.

"Craig seems nice though," Katie winks over the tip of her mug.

"Nice and feisty!"

"Shannon!"

"What? I've been to his fights, he'd clobber you!"

"Fights?" Katie asks.

"Craig, Jay, and Dylan are all into MMA, they don't

fight as often as they used to but still go in from time to time," I explain. "Craig is a blackbelt in Taekwondo and has numerous wins from boxing, too."

"Explains why they're in such good shape," Katie smirks.

It's true, most guys on building sites are, well, round. They eat crap most of the day, despite their job being physical and it shows after some time.

The guys are in such good shape because they, at least, try to take care of themselves.

We lock up and I check my phone to see if Craig has called.

Unknown

I don't like being ignored. Stay away from him.

What the? That has to be a wrong number, right? I try to dial it back, but the phone is switched off. It sounds like a jilted lover, but Craig never had a serious girlfriend, well, not since his early twenties. This can't be about him, then who the hell are they talking about? Weird, I'm over-analysing this, they obviously sent this to the wrong person.

I press delete, a car horn sounds making me jump out of my skin. I look up to see Craig in the van laughing at giving me a mini heart attack.

"You ok, baby?"

"You scared the shit out of me! What are you doing here?" I shove my phone back into the depths of my bag. I won't let him know just yet, it could be an accident, this could not be meant for me. If I get another though, that's a different story.

"I finished up early," he wiggles his eyebrows up and down. A big grin flashes across his face, "come on, get that gorgeous ass in the van. I'm taking you home."

While I'm prepping dinner, Craig is lounging on the couch, freshly showered, and armed with a book. I glance at the cover. The Hobbit. I should have guessed. This must be his third copy since I moved in.

"Craig?" I think it's better if I do tell him about that text message. It's been playing on my mind since I received it. I need to know if it's a possible ex-lover.

"Hmm?" He peeks up over his book.

"You weren't... seeing anyone before we? I mean anything more than a fling?"

"No. Why?"

"It's just— never mind..."

"Lottie," Craig closes the book and rises to his full height. "What happened?"

"I got a weird text earlier. Some random number saying to stay away from him."

"Him? Him who?"

"Him you, I think. I don't know, I found it strange. It must have been a wrong number, right?"

"Has to be. Did they say anything else?"

"No. Just that and when I tried to call the number the phone was off."

"Could it be from that number that's been calling you?"

"I thought that too, but I blocked it."

"We'll keep an eye on it, but it has to be a mix-up. Probably a wrong digit or something. It can't be me. I mean, I have not been with anyone serious in years. The only one I wanted was you," he leans down, kissing me ever so affectionately and I melt to his touch. He's right. It's definitely a mix-up.

* * *

Lottie is curled up on the end of the couch, cocooned under her throw, with a hot water bottle sitting on her lap.

"Well?"

"Nope," she sighs dishearteningly.

"Seriously? Why did they reject it?"

"Apparently it's not what's popular right now."

"Bullshit! It's such a great book!"

"Evidently not that great," unwrapping herself, Lottie stalks into the kitchen.

She has wanted to become a writer for as long as I've known her. She writes on the likes of Chapters and other communities; her stories always get thousands of reads and so many people adore them. Hell, they are not my usual reads, and I can't put them down. Don't even get me started on her characters! They're so well written, so deep, and go far beyond the page. The amount of times I've become one of the characters inside her book is insane. I don't understand this rejection. What's popular right now? Who wants to read the same story told fifty different ways? There is a reason the hits become hits because they're new!

Harry Potter, Lord of the Rings, The Hunger Games, hell even Fifty shades of Grey, that was an indie book that took off because so many people loved it despite no publisher wanting it to begin with.

Lottie is so stupidly talented; it pisses me off that she keeps getting rejected by these publishers despite them telling her work shows promise and to send them in her future work.

Bullshit! It's all bullshit!

I find her in the kitchen, staring out into the dark abyss with the kettle boiling. Wrapping my arms around her, I drop my lips to her neck, inhaling that familiar coconut scent from her hair.

She squeezes my hand and I catch our reflection in the window, she smiles and leans into me.

"It will happen, I know it will. I have faith in you, babe."

"Thank you."

"Look, King got rejected, Rowling got rejected, Tolkien didn't take off properly until after he died."

"That will be my luck," she snorts.

"Lottie, you're so talented, I'm not just saying that because I want to get into your pants."

"So, you don't want to get into my pants?"

"I'd live between your legs if that was an option."

She snorts, turning her head to me, her lips graze my cheek. "Don't ever change, Batman."

LOTTIE

*J*ay and Tiffany invited us out for something to eat after work. Our favourite spot—Tiffy's, and mine. The food here is incredible as usual.

Apparently, there is some 80s, 90s, and 00s night in the pub up the road. It does not take much convincing on Tiffy's behalf before we're tripping over ourselves to get there. Jason and Craig come up the rear, acting as our unofficial bodyguards.

Tiffany, and I dance, shimmying and swaying to the music while the guys lurk at a nearby table. I feel a pair of hands on my hips and turn, *who the hell is this?* Pulling away, the guy clearly not getting the hint tries to move in again

"I'm taken," I growl hoping the words might deter him. They don't.

"It's just a dance," I can feel the heat coming from his alcohol-soaked breath.

"Not interested," glancing at the table the guys were at I can't see Craig or Jay. Maybe they went outside? The guy takes another step towards me. "I said no!"

"Come on, it's my birthday."

"I don't care, piss off."

Tiffy shoves her way in front of me, cutting him off, "listen, dick-for-brains, she said no! Back off!"

"Hey, you don't need to be such a bitch, it was only a bit of fun," his friend chimes in.

"Fun? I said no, you fucking imbecile."

"Got quite the mouth there, don't you."

"Leave us alone," I grab Tiffy and storm out to the smoking area hoping the guys will be out there. I hate playing a damsel in distress but sometimes a girl needs her man to step in and defend her against dickheads like this.

We get outside. No sign of the guys, for an optimistic

minute I'm convinced we lost the two assholes.

I feel a hand grip my arm, hard enough to leave marks. "Let's dance!"

Oh my god! Why are men such scumbags? "Let's not," yanking my arm free, I step back.

"Touch her again and I'll snap your neck," his voice is low, gruff, protective. I breathe a sigh of relief as Craig seemingly appears out of thin air. He's by my side in a heartbeat.

"They're with us, get your own," the guy's friend grunts.

Jay wrenches him forward by his shirt until they're nose to nose. The guy struggles but Jason is clearly stronger than him. "What did you say?"

Craig is already rolling up his sleeves, ready to pounce.

Before I can say anything, the guy in Jason's hold attempts to punch his way free and all hell breaks loose.

A crowd starts to gather, punches fly, kicks, threats, blood.

The two guys are left on the ground. One under a turned-over table, their chests rising and falling so we know they're still alive.

Craig and Jason's chests heave, their knuckles are busted open, nostrils flaring as they look at the guys they practically smashed through the concrete.

Jason turns, scooping Tiffy up and putting her over his shoulder, fleeing the pub. Craig grabs me and we follow, leaving before the garda shows up.

"Craig," I tug, slowing him to a stop once we put enough distance in. I look at his knuckles, busted and bloody, his countenance terrifying to behold. Yet I have to admit watching him just now, how protective he is of me, how dominating he can be, it was a major turn-on. "You're hurt."

"No, I'm not."

"Let's go," Jay insists.

Craig grabs me again, dragging me back to the house.

When we get home, he charges to the bathroom to clean up while Jay goes into the kitchen.

"Craig?"

"He shouldn't have touched you!" he shouts from behind the bathroom door.

Wow, talk about defensive; does he think I'm mad at him?

I charge into the bathroom to confront him, as soon as he turns to me I can see the anxiety behind his eyes. He was worried about me. Hopping up on the counter, taking the hand towel, and running it under the water I reach out, take his wrist, and pull him closer.

Dabbing the towel on his knuckles, "you're sure you're, OK?"

"I'm fine."

I keep dabbing the blood from his hands, squeezing my legs around his waist, "this looks sore."

"It's nothing," he towers over me, strong, dominating, sexy.

Dropping the towel, I reach up and haul him down for a kiss. He growls gripping onto my hips as he pulls me closer. Our mouths compete for the best taste of one another. Raking my nails down his back, fisting the material of his shirt, I yank it overhead. My fingers dance over his sculpted abs as he leans in for another toe-curling kiss.

"Let me take care of you," I kiss his neck and nibble on the whorl of his ear. Sliding off the counter, I lead Craig to the bedroom, pop open the button of his jeans before I push him on the bed and pull them off him.

"Jason and Tiffany are still downstairs," he reminds me.

Hearing a chair scrape across the ground from the floor below I shoot him a knowing look. "Get on your knees and put that mouth of yours to work," Craig growls.

I have never liked the thoughts of being dominated, ever. But Craig— I'll happily submit to him, every single time.

* * *

I try to move but it feels as if my body is tied down by invisible threads. I feel myself growing hard inside her mouth. Her tongue is long and soft. It seems to wrap itself around me.

She keeps up the perfect pace and suction, eager to please, and my God she knows how to please. Just as I'm about to come she suddenly moves away and slowly begins to undress.

"I need to feel you in me," she holds me in one hand while she slides down my length. Lottie's in charge and I like it, she pins my hands down then lets her breasts touch my face. Wrapping my lips around her nipple I suck hard, grazing my teeth over the hardening nub. I'm like a savage; I start to buck. I can't control myself, not with her.

Lottie starts moving her hips, teasing the ever-living hell out of the tip. She rolls her hips once, twice, three times then slams down taking my full length. Breaking free of her hold, my hands roam freely. Gripping that perfect ass, I guide her up and down my length.

* * *

I feel one of his fingers flicking over my ass. I do it to him, if he does something I copy him. Craig rolls me off him and takes me from behind, I push back forcing more of him inside me. Craig groans louder, a noise that sends a delicious shockwave through me. I love hearing him, knowing how much he enjoys me.

His body slams into me, my arms buckle, my face buried into the duvet while he continues to drive into me. I feel a delicious sting, and moan, fisting the sheets beneath me. "You like that, baby? You like when I spank your ass while fucking you, don't you?"

"Yes."

"Yeah?" his hand connects again, another sharp delicious shockwave shoots through me. "Tell me, what do you want me to do to you?"

"Take me any way you want, baby, I'm yours."

I hear a growl.

He spins me on my back drawing my knees high and wide then slides back inside. His lips slam down, his tongue delving into my mouth. Craig seems to drive in deeper, I desperately want to give him a release.

I slide a hand between us, his eyes follow, he watches me pleasure myself for him and I feel his body tense.

Craig calls my name, again and again. I haul him down for a passionate kiss, feeling his body shudder on top of me.

When he opens his eyes, he looks dazed, elated. He tries to pull away, but I tighten my legs around him. I love the feel of him on top of me, I love looking at him.

I forget to tell him at times how much I appreciate him. Craig is my rock. Much like tonight, I know he would never let anyone hurt me.

Pulling his hands to my lips, I press a gentle kiss to each busted knuckle.

"My hero," I smirk. Gazing into his glazed eyes, "we will have to pick a different name, Batman is already taken sadly."

"I still get to keep the cape though, right?"

"Of course," we both laugh, I reluctantly allow him to roll off me. "I'm sorry you got into a fight because of me."

"Lottie, I got into a fight because some asshole was harassing you. It's not your fault. Besides I'm not sorry. I got him away from you, didn't I. You're safe, that's all I care about. No will ever hurt you with me around, baby."

"I know," I roll onto him, snuggling into my personal Craig nook.

"You two want pizza?" Jay calls up the stairs.

"I forgot they were here," I snigger, judging by Craig's wide eyes I was not the only one.

We redress then go downstairs, Tiffy gives me a judgmental stare as we descend the staircase— yeah like she can talk. She has that just fucked hair going on and I heard what was happening in my kitchen while we were upstairs.

Craig turns on Netflix and tosses the remote at Jay. Reclining on the couch, he pulls me down with him and drags a blanket over us both.

Tiffy sits on Jay's lap, her chocolate brown hair shines like glass. She keeps looking over at Craig and me, sniggering every so often.

"What?"

"It's about damn time," she winks at me then turns back to watch the T.V.

We showed up for dinner at Mom's around 5.30, and soon after, we went out for drinks. Mom dragged us to Fibbers, some band was playing that she likes and of course it was all eighties and nineties music.

While mom was chatting up the new bartender, Craig and I were on the dancefloor. Twirling, shimmying, and grinding when dirty dancing songs echoed around the pub.

We got a taxi around two and dropped mom off, then made our way home. We were still pretty wired by the time we were dropped off, ordered kebabs, and ended up watching a nightmare on Elm Street, just because. I don't think we got to bed before five.

I did make a little... erm... oopsies where Nick is concerned. Mom, of course, went snap-happy with the camera and posted everything up on her Facebook. One too many cocktails will do that to her. Ah well, they were up, I knew Nick would see them, so I took my favourite picture of Craig and me together and updated my profile picture. I also changed my status. Talk about blind-sighting Nick. It seemed like a good idea last night but considering, he is on the phone now demanding an explanation I probably should have waited until today before pulling a stunt like that.

* * *

I turn the water off in the shower and hear that Lottie is still on the phone with Nick. Well, I guess that was one way to let him know. He messaged me this morning demanding answers. Like what does he want me to say? It is what it is, and I told him that. He obviously was not too keen on my response and decided to give Lottie the third degree.

Thanks to Lottie a Nightmare on Elm Street is now ruined for me. Completely ruined. It barely started. The camera rolls onto Freddie chasing that girl down the street, and Lottie broke out laughing, I was wondering what was so funny until she went back, told me to keep my eyes on Freddie. That run killed it. No longer scary. It looks like Freddie is about to shit himself with that bow-legged run. He is now added to the list of horror movie characters Lottie took the edge off from. Pennywise is another.

The original IT, it's a classic for a reason. Lottie sat through about five minutes of it and start cackling saying that it sounded like a nan after smoking too many fags. Now I can't unhear it. I thought we would have better luck with the new one and even she said Bill Skarsgard plays the role really well, then I had to buy her the bloody book.

As soon as Pennywise introduces himself as Bob, that's it, he's added to the bench. Bob the killer clown, Lottie made a point of mimicking the dog from Hotel Transylvania three. Now every time I think of it all I hear is, "Hi, Bob."

I shave and go into our room to find Lottie hanging off the bed like a bat, barely listening to Nick. He sounds like he has calmed down, I can just about make him out.

"As long as you're happy..."

"I am."

"Alright, I'll see you when I get back."

"K," Lottie smiles up at me and rolls onto her stomach, pushing herself back onto the bed.

"All good?" I ask after she hangs up.

"It's fine, no shotgun wedding, don't worry," she chortles then falls back to the pillows.

I know Nick is only looking out for her, especially given her track record. Ok, fair enough, mine might not exactly put him at ease either, but Lottie is different than the others. I would never do anything to hurt her.

* * *

Steady drops of water run down his chest and off the ends of his hair framing his face. Craig has a towel wrapped around his middle, he pulls it off and starts drying his hair with it. I cannot help but admire what a fine specimen of a man he is. His steel-grey eyes, handsome face, cheekbones that would cut glass. My eyes roam over him favourably, I've admired him from afar for years but to see him up close and personal like this still shocks me. To be fair, we are still brand new. A little over a week together. Well, four days officially.

I guess you could say that things are moving fast. We have christened every room in the house and exchanged words of devotion already. But we have known each other for so long. We already live together, surely there was no possible way to do this slowly.

I pull myself from the bed and throw on a maxi dress I left hanging up, a way of making an effort without trying too hard. We are to be at Josie's soon. Although I know Josie and we get on quite well, I can't help but feel a little pressured about today. I mean, when I saw her last, I was just Craig's roommate. His friend. Now I'm going in as his lover.

I glance in the mirror, fixing my hair. Craig comes behind me, his head next to mine, his chin on my shoulder. He is smiling at me in the mirror. "Beautiful, as always," I feel his lips graze my cheek, I can't help but smile back.

I have always felt somewhat self-conscious. Don't get me wrong I never thought I looked like the creature from the blue lagoon or anything but just... I don't know... plain, especially compared to some of the glamourous girls I have seen Craig with before. But he doesn't seem to see what I do. His words are always genuine, he makes me feel beautiful.

* * *

My God, she's stunning. We drive to Josie's, despite keeping my eyes fixed ahead I can't keep my hands off Lottie. My hand drops to her knee, her hand on my leg, I'm using her hand to change gears. I can't help it; I have to touch her.

When we pull up to Josie's I let us in and hear nan pottering about the kitchen. "Knob Goblin!"

"Hello to you, too," I walk around the counter, kiss her cheek then look at what caused the outburst. The counter is dusted in flour from where she knocked the bag over. It looks like Tony Montana was having a field day in here. "I'll get that."

"No. Pop the kettle on. Dinner will be ready soon," Josie shoos me away, she looks anxious.

"What's up, buttercup?"

"Nothing."

"Josie, I'm not a chimney, don't blow smoke up my ass," I turn my attention to the oven, it looks like she's cooking for more than just the three of us.

"Expecting someone?"

"I—"

I hear the front door open and immediately step out to see what's going on. I'm the only one bar Josie with keys to this house. "I could not get the half and half; I hope full fat is ok—oh..."

Who the fuck are you? I study the stranger in my family home. He looks in and around Josie's age, possibly older. Clean crisp shirt, perfectly pressed pants, shoes I can see my reflection in.

"Full fat is fine, Craig does not mind, do you?"

"No."

He extends his hand; my gaze falls to it. Josie clears her throat. "Craig, this is George."

"I've heard so much about you. It's nice to finally put a face to the name," his hand still extended.

I feel Lottie's hand slide around my arm, she leans forwards taking George's hand, shaking firmly. "It's nice to meet you, George, I'm Lottie." She subtly stands on my foot, snapping me out of it.

"Yeah, eh..." My eyes flit to Josie, then turn back to George. "Good to meet you."

* * *

Oh dear, I thought we pulled the rug out from under Nick, but this, Craig was not at all prepared for. Safe to say he is not handling the surprise so well. He stalks over to the cupboards, pulls out some glasses then walks out of the room. Only to come back in a few minutes later mumbling under his breath. "Where is your ice?"

"I have none," Josie replies.

"How do you have no ice? Is your freezer broken?"

"No."

"Your water turned off?"

"No."

"Did you forget the recipe?"

125

"Craig," I call in a warning tone. I know he is not responding well to this but there is no need to be an ass about it.

He turns to look at me then retreats from the room.

"Oh dear, he is not taking this well at all, is he?" George sighs.

"He will be fine; I'll go talk to him."

"No, Lottie. It is fine. I should go," Josie tosses the tea towel on the counter and walks out of the room.

* * *

"Are you going to sulk for the rest of the evening?"

I glance up to see Josie standing in the doorway. "I'm not sulking."

"You could have fooled me."

"Who is he?"

Josie sighs then walks over to the bed. My room is exactly the way I left it. She never bothered to change it after I moved out. "George is... my companion."

"Ugh, no stop."

"Craig. I deserve to be happy."

"You are happy!"

"Living alone... can get lonely. I like the company."

"You have me!"

"I understand that this is hard for you. I'm not trying to replace Grandad. No one will ever replace that man. But don't you think that he would want me to find someone?"

"No."

"Why?"

"Because you're old! You're supposed to be... I don't know baking, knitting... get a cat for fuck's sake."

"You're happy with Lottie..."

"That's different," wow, I missed the part when I swallowed a stroppy teenager. Do I really sound like that?

"Because?"

"My balls aren't knocking about my knees!"

"Good for me that I don't have a set."

"Josie!" I beg, trying not to laugh.

Her hair is a perfectly styled ash platinum blonde, makeup is perfectly done. Her bright grey eyes— my mom's grey eyes, sparkling back at me. "Give him a chance, please. For me."

She looks so much like my mom. Timeless, beautiful, mischievous. "Fine. But no funny business!"

* * *

The rest of the evening goes by fine. Craig behaves as best he can. I help Josie with the dishes after everyone is done eating. Craig makes himself scarce when Josie walks George out to say goodbye. I think they're cute together, but I'm not voicing that opinion in front of Craig right now. He'll come around; I know he will. Much like Nick did earlier after the initial shock of it all.

The drive back is nice, it was an early dinner, so when we left Craig decided to take the backroads home. He pulled up in a layby and we watched the sunset before driving home.

I fiddle with my keys, trying to figure out which key is which when I feel my foot kicking something. I look at the ground, there is a small package by the door with my name on it.

We go inside and Craig plops on the couch, pulling me with him.

"Amazon?" He asks, glancing at the parcel.

"No... I didn't order anything."

Tearing open the cardboard, whatever it is covered by paper. I can feel my heart start to pound in my chest. Craig takes the package off me, noticing me tense, and pulls out the contents. There is a picture of me and Craig from the café from last Sunday before we came home. Another of him collecting me from Moms. A picture of Craig on site, his stolen chop saw. Me at work, Us last night in the pub with Mom.

I glance at the note.

This is your final warning. Stay away!

CRAIG

*I*t has been a few weeks since Lottie got the package. We went straight to the police and filed a report, they took the letter and photographs for evidence. We have whoever did it on harassment if nothing else, but wouldn't you know, as soon as we went to the police the letters and texts stopped coming in.

The sick bastard must have got spooked. Good. They want to worry more about what I'll do to them if I ever find out who did it. Poor Lottie was in a cruel state. I had to speak with the landlord about installing a house alarm and camera at the front door, just in case. They were fine with it. Helps cover them and I was the one paying for it.

In truth, I could have moved out years ago. I have more than enough put aside to build my own place. Lottie is the reason I stayed. The reason I haven't left renting behind me. If I leave here I'm taking her with me but it's too soon— technically speaking. We are together a wet weekend. Sure, we already live together. Have done for years but getting our own place? Like ours, not anyone else's, it seems like a big step and although I'm all in, I'm afraid that it might be too fast for her. Given how jumpy she has been as of late I don't want to scare her.

We have been to numerous dinners and lunches with Josie and George. I'm getting used to it. It's still weird though, my nan starts dating at the same time as me? I don't even want to think of what that entails. Josie came out with 'you're never too old for sex' at lunch the other day. No. Apparently, you're never too old to be traumatised by the idea of it either. Of course, Lottie found this hilarious.

I come in from work to find Lottie stretched out over the couch.

"What you got there?"

She closes the book without the bookmark, I take it she's just finished. I recognise the cover as one from the bookstore she picked up a few weeks ago.

"Blood Orange," covering her mouth as she yawns, she then stretches out her limbs and debates sitting up or staying put.

"Sum it up in five words or less."

"It's about a strangle wank."

I pause halfway between the stairs and the kitchen. "Any batman suits?"

"Afraid not."

"Then I'm not interested."

I hear her grunt and the noise of the fabric rustling from the blanket she cocooned in. "I was talking to Katie today," her voice follows me into the kitchen.

Lottie has a lasagne cooking away in the oven, I catch a glimpse of it when I walk past. I love her cooking. None of that readymade, store-bought shit. Everything Lottie makes she does it by hand.

"Oh yeah?"

"Yeah. She noticed I seemed drained a lot more often lately..."

Well, that's true. But I put that down to the aftermath of Nick's wedding, our late nights up, and of course, that arsehole trying to scare her.

"She thinks I may be deficient in some vitamins, so I booked myself in with the doctor for some blood tests to be safe."

"Not a bad idea. You could just be run down though, babe. With everything that happened."

"True, better safe than sorry, I suppose."

"You're definitely off, Tuesday and Wednesday yeah?" I ask, turning to see her approach. I pull her to me by the hips and she giggles.

"Yeah, why?"

"I booked us into the Monart. Some time away would

be nice. No family dinners. No phones. Plus, it's a kid-free hotel so we don't have to listen to other people's kids throwing mickey fits for the two days."

"I told you not to spoil me."

"It's for me, too," not a total lie. It does look like a good break away.

"Can we afford it? That's a five-star place, right?"

"It is. We can. It's all arranged. Besides, I got a good midweek deal, one treatment each, dinner and breakfast included."

"I don't even want to know how much that cost."

"Not as much as you think."

She looks tired. The house is spotless, the dinner is on, judging by the timer it will be ready soon enough. Maybe I should put her to bed soon? I sound like a parent. The vitamin deficiency is plausible, at the same time I think she might be run down. Even the other night when I got in, we had dinner. I cleaned up and Lottie went upstairs to watch some True Crime thing on Netflix. I crawled in beside her hoping to get something going, she seemed into it too, until I noticed she wasn't as attentive as usual. I pulled away from her neck to notice her eyes were closed, she was not asleep yet, semi-conscious more like it. That was enough for me to put the brakes on and spend the rest of the night ignoring a semi.

* * *

My boy did good. I have absolutely no problem in saying it, this place is incredible. No clothing, except for dinner. They encourage you to walk around in your robe and swimwear all day! I love this place. Even pulling up was amazing, a valet as soon as we drove up, bags were brought in and taken to the room. We got the full tour on check-in and oh, my God, I want to live here!

We barely get in the door and it's already sooooo

relaxing. We are shown the bar and restaurant, the gym, salons, and the spa itself. So many rooms. The sauna, steam rooms, some weird, heated chair room, another steamy salt room thing, I'm not really sure what that's called but I know where I'm going when I change! They have an outdoor sauna, a swimming pool, and then the treatment rooms. Heaven.

They have all these flavoured, detox waters laid out between the sauna, steam rooms, and the swimming pool and I wouldn't even mind, I thought it would just be a normal hotel swimming pool. No! this has a walled-off jacuzzi section and this waterfall effect shower thing that shoots down on you in the pool. They have this wide-open widow view that you can see directly into the gardens while reclining on heated ceramic loungers.

The room is gorgeous, and the bathroom is huge, we even have our own balcony overlooking the gardens. I'm not going home. I am staying here.

I'm so excited to get started, I check my phone when we get to the room, it went off when we were being checked in and given the tour. I did not want to be rude so I put the phone on silent. It's probably just mom making sure that we got here ok.

Two messages and one missed call. Mom. No surprise there, I send her a text to say we got here safe, and I'll call her later. Then I check the other message. A notification from the missed call. My Doctor's office. I had my blood tests done on Tuesday last week the results must have come in. I walk out to the balcony and call her back while Craig is changing.

* * *

I have to thank Josie for telling me about this place. This is incredible. I don't know what I thought a spa weekend would be like but I'm already warming up to it. I'm glad I decided to go with jeans instead of the tracksuit bottoms. Imagine pulling up at a place like this in a tracksuit?

I look around the room, the staff left some chocolates out for us, and a bottle of champagne I pre-arranged for the room is set out with them. While I wait on Lottie, I crack the champagne open and pour two glasses, then go to the wardrobe and pull out the robes and slippers. I hear Lottie step back in and turn, she's as white as a sheet.

"You ok, baby?"

"Yeah," her voice barely audible.

"What happened?"

Lottie glances at the champagne, then the bed. She chooses the bed, sitting down slowly.

"Baby? What did the doctor say?" I kneel at her feet and look up at her, she looks out of it. The fact that she's not saying anything isn't helping. I'm starting to freak out. What the hell could be wrong with her? What did the blood tests show? Is she sick? As I run through a list in my mind, Lottie speaks. I almost miss it. "I'm sorry, what?"

"I'm pregnant." It still doesn't register. She's looking at me, searching me for a reaction. I'm too busy wondering what the hell I just heard. Pregnant? That can't be right, can it? She didn't just tell me— "Craig?"

"Pregnant?"

She nods in response.

* * *

Oh my God, he's freaking out. I can't say I blame him. It's barely registered with me as it is. Pregnant. I'm pregnant. With Craig's baby. All I can hear is the blood pumping past my ears. All I can see is Craig wide-eyed, on his knees, looking as if he might topple over.

He slowly pushes himself to his full height and I find myself mirroring his actions on instinct.

"Craig?" I try again. He blinks rapidly, mouth ajar.

Then he looks at me. A smile slowly stretching across his face. Without saying a word, I'm airborne. He has me in his grasp and is twirling me around the room. "You're pregnant!" This time it's not a question. He's cheering it. "We're having a baby?" He puts me on my feet, beaming. It's like a weight has been lifted from my shoulders. He doesn't seem angry or upset at all. He seems ecstatic.

"We are," I gift him a large toothy grin, his lips come down on mine.

* * *

The champagne in the room got a death. I drank the bottle. I was shaking like a leaf and needed something to steady my nerves. Lottie's pregnant! I'm going to be a father. That's fucking terrifying. Lottie is going to be the mother of my child; I could not ask for anything better. I hit the jackpot with her. She will be a great mom, I know it.

We check with the girls in the spa about what is safe for Lottie to use. Safe to say my thoughts of getting sexy in the jacuzzi went up in smoke. But that's fine. It's not about me. It's about Lottie. Lottie and the baby. My baby.

Holy crap this does not feel real.

If it were any other girl, I'd have probably jumped out the fucking window by now, but with Lottie, I don't know, it's still terrifying but in a good way. It's an adventure I want to take with her. Starting our own little family together. I know it's fast, but it's not like we just met. I've known Lottie for years. Loved her for years. So, what if our relationship, as such, is new.

We spend most of the day in the pool, and that weird salt room Lottie likes. Then to our individual massages and meet up in the darkroom after.

At dinner, we indulge a bit too much. Lottie is happy with her virgin cocktails, trying at least one of every kind, then can't decide between the desserts, so we end up ordering two each. Lottie decides she wants my sticky toffee pudding in place of her brownie, and I don't argue. She has my kid in there, whatever she wants, she gets. No questions asked.

She is in a food coma as soon as we get back to the room. As I hold her close, I can't help but think of how much my life has changed in the space of a few weeks. If you told me three months ago that I would be here, on a spa day with Lottie and that she would be pregnant with my baby, I would have told you to get your head checked. She was the girl I could never have, the one just out of reach. Now she's mine, she's mine and this beautiful woman is having my baby.

I like to think that my mom has something to do with this. She would have loved Lottie. Sadly, they never got a chance to meet, that my baby will never know their nanny, but at least I'll have someone watching over them, over us. And let's not forget, they'll always have Josie.

Josie. I can't wait to tell her. But we agreed to wait until we get back and go get the scan to make sure everything is as it is supposed to be before telling anyone.

I want to tell everyone.

I'll need to get baby things in, baby proof the house... maybe... maybe I can talk Lottie into moving out? Into getting our own house. There is enough time, I have the money. I have the land, planning permission. It takes roughly seven months to build a house from start to finish, it's pushing it a bit close but at least it will be ours. Worst case scenario, the baby is a few months old before we move.

Lottie sighs and snuggles in closer to me, I glance at her sleeping peacefully. It's going to work. Our baby. Our house. Our family. A fresh start.

LOTTIE

*W*e spent the last day of our stay in pure relaxation.
Breakfast was amazing, they had a massive set up of fresh
fruits, pastries, juices, tea, coffee, cereal, etc, and to top it
all off we could also order anything off the menu. I feasted.
I've been ravenous lately. I'll be the size of a house by the
time this child is born if this is the way my pregnancy is
going to go.

While Craig had a quick stint in the sauna, I was
lounging in the pool like a content little seal. I kept
picturing what our baby will look like, will they have Craig's
big steel grey eyes? My curly auburn hair? Will they have
their daddy's cheekbones? I was so nervous after getting
the call yesterday, but the more I think about it, the more I
realise that I've nothing to fear, not really.

Well, there is the birth, I'm petrified of that, I'm crap
with pain. I'm a wimp. In general, though, having Craig as
my partner, having him as the father of my child, I could
not ask for anything better.

Attraction aside, he is an amazing role model for our
little one. He works so hard, built his business up from the
ground up, he is by no means rich, but he is comfortable
financially. Not scraping by from one end of the month to
the next like I am. I mean, my job pays well I suppose, but
two weeks after payday and once all the bills are taken out,
I'm broke. I've to make two hundred last me the rest of the
month and that's including bus fare back and forth to work,
lunch, food shopping. In truth, I needed a roommate a hell
of a lot more than Craig ever did.

I feel bad in a way though, I can't wait to tell mom.
She's going to be over the moon, her first grandchild. I just
hate the fact that Craig does not get to share this with his
mother. Although I'm sure Josie will make up for it. I can
only imagine her reaction when we tell her.

Craig booked me in for a pregnancy massage before we left, and I went a bit stab happy at dinner. I couldn't help it; the food was amazing. I made sure to order both the sticky toffee pudding and cheesecake because I needed them in my life. Craig just laughed, probably happy that I didn't steal his dessert this time.

I wonder how far along I am. It's hard to tell really. I've always been irregular. Nothing seemed amiss, I assumed that when I got a light bit of bleeding last month that that was my period, apparently it was breakthrough bleeding.

* * *

"Congratulations," Jay slaps me on the back when I announce it. I have the scan picture in my wallet. Lottie has the rest. This tiny little peanut is our baby. They reckon she is about eight weeks along.

Kim practically rugby tackled me when she found out. I never thought I'd see her that excited but by God, she could put a banshee to shame with that squeal.

Nick was pretty happy about it, a little pissed that we got there before him and Abbie but all and all it went pretty smoothly.

Josie— I made the mistake of telling her when she was emptying the dishwasher, safe to say she will need new plates, wine glasses, whatever else was in there. Josie is ecstatic. She immediately glued her hand to Lottie's belly despite the fact she's not even showing yet. I had to tell her that she won't get three wishes for rubbing Lottie.

It's exciting, surreal even. Seeing our baby on the screen, hearing their heartbeat. I'm going to be someone's dad. I'll be a much better one than the one I had. I'll never let that kid be without me.

Lottie has herself slung over the dining chair and is devouring the last of the ribs while reclining.

"Did you just do what I thought you did?" looking at

the open jar of honey and Lottie's sticky fingers, I'm sure she just dipped the meat in there.

"Yep. It's massive, you should try it sometime," Lottie smirks, proceeding to suck the remaining meat off the bone.

"Just the one baby in there?"

"Yep. Oh, that reminds me, I hope you're prepared for the aftermath. Apparently, blood clots are a bitch according to Shannon," swivelling herself around in the chair so she is sitting upright, Lottie reaches for the glass in front of her.

"Blood clots?"

"Mmm, hmm," Lottie sucks on her teeth trying to remove a piece of meat stuck between them. "Piles too, Shannon said it was like smuggling a bunch of grapes up her a—"

"Babe! I'm trying to eat here."

"Ah, go ask my arse," giving up her attempts to suck out the piece of meat, Lottie goes in with her nail to dig it out instead.

"Why should I be prepared for this anyway?"

"Because I'm going to be very sore, and probably traumatised every time I need to use the bathroom. At least for a few weeks."

"We have a while to worry about that yet, doll."

"Still. I'd like to be prepared. I'm going in with the thoughts of my ass exploding in the labour ward."

"Preparing yourself by psyching yourself out?"

"Meh," she shrugs, then frowns. "Any more milk?"

"Heartburn again?"

"Yep. Mom said that's a sign of the baby having a lot of hair. At this rate, I'm going to birth Chewbacca."

* * *

It's been another, long day on-site, our site. Construction has started on our house. I'm there every chance I get and the lads on the roster help out when they can. It's handy having so many working for us. Most are more than happy to pick up the odd nixer.

Lottie is pacing up and down the bedroom, not long out of the shower.

"Come to bed, baby."

"Fine. But I want you to do something for me."

I arch an eyebrow, biting my lower lip as I take her measure. "Anything you want, love."

She climbs onto the bed. I kiss her neck and she sighs. "Read me to sleep, I'm too tired to do it myself."

Feeling myself deflate, I filter the air out my nostrils. "I was hoping for something more... sensual."

"Do what you want when I'm asleep just don't wake me."

"Come here then," holding the book out in front of us, I snake my arm around Lottie's waist, in slow stroking motions, I find my hand wandering.

"Craig!"

"Sorry. Can't help it,"

* * *

Craig reads to me. Flicking over the page he gets halfway down when I ask him one too many questions about his book.

"You know what," Craig slams the book shut and reaches over for one of mine. "Let's try one of— this is smut."

"It's romance."

"It's badly written smut, babe."

"Just read..."

"Look he barely puts the tip in and she's moaning! What has she got a vibrator shoved up there that it failed to mention?"

I curl up laughing into his chest.

"No foreplay, he just slides in? That would be like striking a match."

"It's fiction, it doesn't have to make perfect sense."

"Obviously, he must have about eight hands for this shit."

"I love you," I manage to get out in between breaths.

I knew he would react like this, he is the person that pointed out that fifty shades of grey is only romantic because the male protagonist is loaded. "If he were a guy at the Tesco checkouts, you'd be out the window calling the guards after seeing his playroom. I've seen enough criminal minds to know red flags when I see them." Of course, I couldn't argue with his logic.

He's right as always. I felt like crap today, had my first spell of morning sickness and I'm never eating wheatbix again. It was like cement coming back up. The reflux is killing me, yet no matter how crap I feel, Craig always manages to make me smile, to laugh.

I reach up, guiding his face to mine with the tips of my fingers, and kiss him. Suddenly, I'm awake. My hormones are going crazy.

"I thought you were tired?" He growls as I slide my hand inside the band of his boxers.

"Second wind," I smile, rolling on top of him, he sends the book across the room.

"You know what I love about you being pregnant?" he bites down on his lip, his gaze raking over me favourably.

"The bigger tits?"

"No condoms," Craig tosses me on my back before I can blink.

CRAIG

I have no idea how I ended up here. I've no idea how she got me to do it. But I'm babysitting Carter, Shannon's young lad, while the girls are gone out.

I don't know what to do with a toddler. Talk about throwing me in the deep end. I figure as long as he is breathing when Shannon comes back then I did well.

My phone vibrates in my pocket and I check the text.

Lottie

All good batman? xx

You

All good here babe xxx

I snap a picture of Carter so they know I haven't lost him yet and send it on through.

The sitting room looks like a bomb went off, I guess this will be my reality soon enough. Toys everywhere. I tried to clean up but as soon as Carter caught me, he toppled out his toy boxes, and everything was spread back out again.

He's a good kid. All I've been made do is sit down, watch Disney movies and play cars. It's not much different than entertaining Lottie.

I gave him a cookie, the big kind from Lidl and now we're best friends.

My phone rings, caller unknown.

"Hello?"

"Leave," the voice rasps on the other side of the phone.

"What?"

"Leave her."

"Who is this?"

"I won't ask again!"

Carter runs over and hands me a plunger. I've no idea where he pulled this from, so I get up to put it back in the bathroom.

"Jay? Is this you you tit? What are you playing at?" I laugh over the phone, the wrong thing to do, whoever is on the other end is livid. It just makes it that much more entertaining.

"Do you want me to come over there?"

"That depends. Do you want to be impaled by a suction cup?" I put the plunger down and turn out of the bathroom. Carter is bouncing around to Thunderstruck. I love this kid.

"Watch your back, Barnes." The voice sounds put on, like a bad version of Ghostface. If they're going for intimidating they have missed the mark by a mile.

"But my front is so much more appealing wouldn't you say?"

They hang up.

Damn. I was hoping to milk that a bit more.

Still, that was a bit weird all the same. I wonder if it's the same person who sent the pictures a few weeks ago?

I'm not telling Lottie. She doesn't need to be worrying about some schoolyard scare tactics, especially now. I shoot Nick a quick text to see what he thinks. He is a cop after all.

He rings back almost instantly.

"Yeah?"

Nick wastes no time getting into it, "what did they say?"

"Just to leave Lottie."

"What did you say?" His voice sounds strained like even this is now grating on him. Lottie is his sister after all.

"Kind of laughed at them."

"Anything else?"

"They threatened to come over here."

"Your response?"

"To shove a plunger up his ass."

Nick snorts, then clears his throat, trying to remain somewhat professional. "So it's definitely a guy?"

"Yeah. I can think of one off the top of my head. A cheating ex with a bad temper, someone entitled that thinks of Lottie as property."

"Michael."

"Hey, would you look at that, great minds think alike."

"How would he get your number though?"

"I use the same phone for work as I do personal shit. It's easy to get."

"True. Ok, well given the photos, texts to Lottie, and notes. Now, this. We have the fucker on harassment and stalking. The only problem is proving it's him."

"Let him show up. I'll happily use the plunger."

"That's assault."

"Nope. It's not, it's self-defence if he breaks in."

Nick goes quiet for a minute, then says, "You thought a little bit too much about this."

I shrug, "can you blame me?"

"Not in the slightest. If it is Michael... he's a coward. I don't think you have to worry too much about the threat."

"I wasn't worried. I'm not telling Lottie."

"No, don't. She will only worry about it. Keep this between us. Log this call for your own sake and any other you might receive. The more we have on the bastard, the better our chances of charges sticking come an arrest. I can't do much, bar bring him in for questioning without something solid to go on. I'd love to stick someone on him for a while but I can't."

Not a bad idea. "Right, I better get back to Carter."

"Ok, man, talk to you later."

I swipe up on my contacts, searching for a name. The phone rings three times before they answer.

"Hello?"

"Hey, it's me. That favour you owe me, I'm calling it

in."

* * *

I was upstairs putting clothes away when I heard Craig talking on the phone downstairs. Do you ever get those times when you're genuinely not listening to someone but one phrase or word and suddenly you find yourself eavesdropping? Yeah, that's me right now.

"Well, you do have a really sexy voice..." I hear him laughing and pacing around downstairs. Then another laugh. "Ooh yeah, I like it rough!" Another booming laugh. "Yeah? Well, if you're that desperate to see me, come by the site tomorrow. I'll make sure we have some time alone."

I listen for a minute, the call seems to be over.

"Who was that?" I step out on the landing and he spins to see me.

"Huh?" There is something unreadable on his face as he looks at me. "Just Jay."

"Jay is desperate to see you despite you only getting in from work?"

"Err... yeah."

"What's going on?" I can't believe he is blatantly lying to my face! It was obviously not Jay who was on the other end of that call. What the hell is he hiding?

"Nothing."

"You're very defensive right now."

"Not at all, that's just your hormones, babe."

* * *

I hate lying to Lottie, but what am I supposed to say? Oh, that was just that arsehole trying to scare me away from you. By the way, Nick and I think that it's your psycho ex.

I can't risk it. The stress of that could not only hurt

Lottie but our baby.

If Michael wants to get to me so badly he can come and face me like a man. I will not allow him to terrorise my family.

We got new scan pictures today. I take the one I put in my wallet out to look at it.

"Whatcha doing?" Lottie asks, descending the staircase.

"Looking at peanut."

"Peanut?"

"Well, we don't know if it's a boy or girl so, yeah, peanut."

"It's crazy how much they've changed in a few weeks."

"I know..." I turn to look at her. This amazing woman is sacrificing her body to bring my child into the world. She's already glowing. "I love you," I place my hand on her belly and kiss her head. She smells like coconut. "Both of you."

"We love you, too."

* * *

I'm put at ease the second he wraps his arms around me. Sure that phone call seemed weird. I don't really believe that it was Jason on the other end of the phone.

Perhaps it's my past with Michael and his cheating that made me doubt Craig? I don't know what that phone call was about but I know Craig. He would never betray me, not when I'm carrying his child, not when he's so determined to build us our own family home.

Still... it doesn't explain his defensive behaviour when I asked him about it. I'm most likely just being paranoid. I don't have anything to worry about with Craig, do I?

LOTTIE

*J*ay is shirtless in the ring with another man, their fists up as they dance around each other. The ring is the place where Craig and Jason take up years of pent-up aggression and pain and cause immense suffering. It is the place they come to vent, to reset. A place to be primitive and not need to worry about another arrest for them lashing out.

Craig and I are on the sidelines with Tiffy, Shannon, and some of the guys that work for Craig and Jason. Dylan is just ahead, with a towel for Jay.

Jason's body jolts with ferocity and unused rage, his body glistening with sweat. Tiffy looks on with proud eyes at her man whose hands are up, protecting his face from incoming strikes. Jay is built like the side of a barn, his opponent may be faster, but one good hit from Jason and the fight will be over.

His opponent dances back and forth on the balls of his feet.

"Come on, Jason!" Craig shouts words of encouragement to his friend. Tiffy is practically fanning herself down, watching the fight unfold.

His opponent swings and misses, he swings again, hitting nothing but air. His fist swings in from the side, striking Jay in the jaw. Spittle flies from Jay's mouth, but he is not deterred. Jay's knee comes up and he kicks out, sending his opponent across the ring.

The man rolls to his feet, winded, but determined to press on. Jason deflects a fist travelling for his gut and repays it with one of his own, his fist connects with his challenger's jaw, putting his full body weight behind it. As soon as the strike connects we know he has won.

"That's my man!" Tiffy squeals.

Jason walks to Dylan, wiping himself down with the towel as his opponent is being carried from the ring. His eyes narrow when he spots Michael entering the gym.

I turn to see who he's looking at and freeze. Craig notices immediately, stepping in front of me like the Alpha male he is.

"What's he doing here? He doesn't fight," I beg.

Michael is wearing a pair of old sweatpants— I know they are old because I remember him wearing them around the house when we were together. He drops a large gym bag by the wall and stretches his arms out in front of him.

"Ignore him, baby. He won't come over here," Craig leans down, kissing me tenderly.

"Barnes, you're next!" One of the trainers call. Glancing at the ring, Craig grins. Pulling his shirt overhead, I hear the approving gasps from the other female spectators. All ogling my man like he's a snack— they can piss off.

I hate that he can eat so much crap and still look like an underwear model. I eat a slice of toast and I resemble the Pillsbury doughboy!

Craig hands his shirt to me and steps into the ring. His grey eyes sparkle maliciously as he locks eyes with Michael, daring him to step in the ring.

As soon as they get the word to go, Craig's opponent moves in, hoping for a quick victory. He throws a punch, then another. Craig expertly ducks and weaves himself out of the way, making his opponent come to him. A fist flies at Craig's head, he deflects and stikes back, once in the gut, then the next strike hits his opponent's chin.

The man hits the ground with a sickening thud, lying sprawled out in the centre of the ring. Craig has barely broken a sweat.

"When the hell did you learn to do that?" Shannon stares at him flabbergasted as he pulls on his shirt.

"Years of practice."

Reaching out, he draws me to his side, then pulls out his phone and poses for a selfie. He continues to kiss and nuzzle me the entire time, his hands resting on my belly.

"Barnes, I believe congratulations are in order," one of the trainers comes over, slapping Craig on the back. "Is this her?"

"This is her," Craig pulls me closer. "Lottie, this is Declan."

"It's nice to meet you," I reach out, shaking his hand. He is just as built as the rest of the guys, I put him around his early forties, big bald head, kind of looks like a council estate version of Vin Diesel.

"What's a girl like you doing with an ugly sod like this?"

"Hey! That's my man you're talking about."

"When are you due?"

I catch Michael's head snapping in our direction. He's clearly eavesdropping.

"March tenth, give or take."

"That will be on you before you know it," Declan chuckles. "Congratulations to you both."

"Thank you."

I leave with Shannon, abandoning the guys back at the gym. I'm knackered, my bed is calling me.

"I didn't know Craig could fight like that?" She presses.

"He's been doing that for years, ever since his mom died. Bobby put him into boxing and Taekwando to help channel the aggression he had towards his dad. The boxing turned into MMA. He used to train twice and three times a week, but he's been so busy with work that he only gets to the gym once a fortnight if he's lucky."

"Did you see Michael's face? It looked like he was about to pee his pants."

"Michael would never do anything with Craig around."

"Definitely not, Craig would obliterate him."

Shannon drops me off, and after I search the presses for snacks, I go up to bed, fully prepared to go to sleep but my hormones have other ideas. They're driving me crazy and Craig is still at the gym.

I go to my old room, find my goodie drawer and get what I'm looking for. I haven't needed this in months, not since Craig and I got together, but desperate times and all that jazz.

Stripping down, getting nice and comfortable on the bed, I turn the vibrator on. Getting into a rhythm, it's not long before I feel myself getting closer.

"AHHHHHH!!!!"

The door opens and I panic, almost jumping from the bed, sending my toy through the air. The noise of my toy shaking across the floor is drowned out by Craig's booming laughter. "You were at the gym!!!"

"I left early," he manages to get out between breaths. Stepping for the vibrator, he picks it up. "Couldn't wait for me, no?"

I imagine my face is the same colour as my hair. I have no comeback, there is no denying what he caught me doing or the fact that he was just attacked by a flying sex toy.

Craig switches off the vibrator and places it on the bed. "Next time, wait for me," his lips ghost mine, then he gets up and walks out of the room. I hear the shower running a few minutes later while I'm still catching my breath.

* * *

I can't believe that she threw a vibrator at my head. I don't know which is funnier, Lottie's reaction when I caught her, or the vibrator bouncing along the floor at high speed.

Just before I step into the shower I notice my phone buzzing by the sink.

"Yeah?"

"Explain yourself," Nick demands.

"Excuse me?"

"Michael has just been down at the station to log a complaint. You threatened to flay him?"

"I've no idea what you're talking about."

"Craig..." there is an obvious warning to his tone.

"I was never alone with Michael, ask Jay and Dylan." They blocked off the exits.

"Awfully convenient that he was threatened in a part of the gym that has no camera," Nick growls.

"So, what you're saying is there is nothing to back up his tall tales."

"I can make this one go away, Craig. But be careful. Stay away from Michael."

"I never went near him."

"Hypothetically speaking," I hear Nick sigh.

"Hypothetically speaking, if I did go near Michael we all know why that would happen." I can feel the rage surging through me at the mention of that asshat.

"I wouldn't blame you for having a few words based on our suspicions but you cannot play vigilante either."

"Damn, no batman suit then?"

"I'm serious!"

"Me too. I think I'd look great in a cape."

"Just— don't do anything stupid."

"I can't promise that."

"Why not?"

"When it comes to Lottie stupid is in my nature."

"Behave yourself."

"Yes, mother," I say smarmily as I end the call.

The little weasel went straight to the cops. You'd swear I actually laid a hand on him. *I didn't.* Tempted as I was. I simply told him to leave Lottie alone and stop the scare-mongering or he'd be using his teeth as painkillers. I think he got my message.

"Who was that?" I didn't even see her in the doorway. How much did she hear?

"Josie."

"You were talking to Josie about a batman suit?" Ok, she caught the end of the conversation, not too bad.

"I think I'd look good in one."

"You're being weird again."

"Maybe it's because someone tossed a plastic bullet at my head."

"oh my— get over it!" She blushes. Still mortified I caught her.

"So, are you just going to stand there, or are you going to join me?" I pull back the shower curtain and wait. Her eyes roam over me, trying to figure out what I'm up to. After a long pause, Lottie sighs then drops her robe, and steps into the shower. "Hey, if I get a batman suit then what are we getting you? Catwoman comes to mind."

"How about poison Ivy?"

"Ooh, I like it! Ooh, both!"

"You need to calm down before you hurt yourself."

"Too late, the image is in my head," I climb in after her, pressing myself up against her.

"Craig..." she giggles, feeling the hard evidence of my desire for her pushing into her back.

"Plastic is no substitute for a good chunk of wood!"

"Craig!" She squeals. I spin her and pick her up, pressing her against the wall.

One thing I've learned since being with Lottie— shower sex is a hazard, but a fun one. We slide left and right, the damp tiled wall does nothing to help. Both of us end up sitting in the bath with the water pouring down on us, to prevent a trip to A&E.

I go to sleep with Lottie in my arms. Knowing that I will do everything in my power to protect her and my child. I may have to lie to her for now, but it's for her own good. I can't have her panicking and looking over her shoulder every five minutes.

Men like Michael thrive on picking on women. It's a different story when they're face to face with another man. Michael learned today that you don't threaten my family and get away with it.

I pull her in closer to me and put my hand on her belly. Pretty soon, I'll be feeling our baby kick. I can't wait.

LOTTIE

Craig has been working his arse off lately. I scoured the net looking for things I could do for him, Craig is always spoiling me, I wanted to return the favour. I got him a day out paintballing with the guys followed by a game of bowling.

The time he is out of the house gives me a chance to prep dinner for him tonight. I'm trying to put some effort in, so I'm making Greek roast lamb for dinner and chocolate lava cake for dessert.

Craig is such a doting father already. He makes sure to have every doctor and hospital appointment off work, he decided that he is going to make the baby's crib rather than buy one.

Craig takes every opportunity to brag that his balls work, which is typical for him. He never seems to be serious with anyone except me, not even Josie. They speak fluent sarcasm. I'm just lucky enough that sarcasm is my first language.

I let myself daydream about our little family. I can't even call it a fantasy because it's our reality. We created this, this amazing little person growing in me. They are half me and half Craig. We are bonded for life because of our baby.

If it's a boy, I can imagine them chasing around a football, screaming at each other playing Mario kart, or going to do the shopping in matching superhero outfits.

If it's a girl, I can imagine her being daddy's little Princess. Craig will have her spoiled. Probably go as far as buying her a pony. I would not put it past him. God forbid anyone tries to date her when she hits puberty. Not only will the poor sod have to worry about Craig but "Uncle Jay," too. That scene from bad boys two comes to mind.

My phone rings, I check the name to be safe. It's Craig.

"Hey, how's it going?" I can't help but smile.

"Good, baby, all good here. Eh... we don't have one of those doughnut things you sit on, do we?"

"Jay shot you in the ass, didn't he?"

"Twice!"

"You'll be feeling that tomorrow," I snort, then turn for my cuppa, and a Maltesers bar. A writer has to have her snacks.

"I'm feeling it now!"

"Aww, should I rub it better?"

"Ooh, yes please!" he is practically purring over the phone. I can imagine him on the other end with that broad dimpled grin.

"Have you just finished up?"

"About twenty minutes ago. Just stopped off to get something to eat before we head to bowling. Is everything ok in the house?"

"Yeah, why wouldn't it be?"

"I hope you're taking it easy."

"I'm not working too hard, don't worry. Dinner is already on and I just want to toss some bits in the attic—"

"No. Do not go up there!" his tone is gruff, sexy.

"Hiding a dead body?"

"We haven't got stairs, Lottie. I'm not having you climbing a rickety ladder to get into the attic. Leave it for me, I'll do it when I get home." Craig rarely calls me by name. He usually means business when he does. I suppose he does have a point.

"Fine. I'll be a damsel for once. You happy?"

"Happy? My arse is killing me!"

"I've to push a baby out in three and a half months."

"Touche. You're ok though? No nausea? Heartburn?"

"No nausea but the heartburn is a given."

"Do you need me to pick up anything?"

"Nope. I'm all stocked up, Batman."

"You're sure?"

"Positive."

"Ok, if you think of anything, let me know and I'll pick it up on my way home."

"I will do."

"Ok, I better go. Love you, baby."

"Love you, too!"

* * *

"How're things going?" Jay asks, biting into his big mac.

"Good. Great actually, pregnancy is treating her well. I've heard horror stories about constant puking and mood swings, but not Lottie. Not yet anyway."

"You're lucky. My sister was a demon when she was pregnant, couldn't say boo and she would punch the head off you," Dylan chuckles.

"Yeah? Lottie's good though, tired more often, and maybe a bit weepy at times but nothing over the top." My phone rings, instinctively I think it's Lottie until I look at the name. "Josie, my auld flower!"

"There's my favourite, grandson!"

"Your only grandson."

"Trust you to spoil the moment."

I hear Jason chuckling lowly beside me.

"What can I do for you?" I ask around a mouthful of burger.

"I was thinking—"

"A dangerous thing for you to do..."

"You're not too old to go over my knee, Craig Barnes!"

"I might enjoy that."

Dylan snorts.

"You need to sort yourself out, son," Josie retorts.

I can't hold in the laugh.

"That ring, Craig..." she continues.

I notice Jay and Dylan's heads snapping towards me.

"Hold on a sec..." I walk away, feeling Jason burning a hole in the back of my head. "What about the ring?"

"Use mine."

"Sorry?"

"My ring. Give it to Lottie," she sounds determined.

"Josie... I... I can't do that."

"Why not?"

"Because it's your ring! Bobby got you that ring, I can't take that from you." Thirty years they were married before he died. I still catch her sliding it on from time to time.

"I don't wear it. I haven't worn it since we got married. It is a beautiful ring. I know Lottie has admired it on more than one occasion."

Yeah, no wonder, it's a fucking sapphire. "Nan, I—"

"I want you to have it, Craig. I know Bobby would want the same."

"But... I... it's— Nan..."

"Craig. I want you to have it. Give it to the girl you love. She deserves it. The ring is better on her hand than gathering dust in my old jewellery box."

"Are you sure?"

"Certain."

"Thank you."

"I'll see you tomorrow for dinner?"

"Yeah, we'll be there."

When I get back to Jason, and Dylan they're both staring at me, demanding an explanation. "Ring?" Jay presses.

"Huh?"

"A ring?" he repeats.

"No idea what you're talking about."

* * *

Craig loads up the dishwasher after dinner. I stare at the flowers he brought home for me. He is so good to me, I am truly blessed to have him.

Little does he know that I have a surprise of my own for him.

I go upstairs and prepare a bath while he is distracted, sprinkle in some rose petals and light some candles, then call him up.

"What's all this?" He asks, wide-eyed.

"Something to take the sting out of your arse."

Craig strips down and climbs into the bath, I follow soon after, resting my head on his chest. The water sloshes around us as he brushes my hair to one side and rests his head against mine. "I've never been one for baths but I have to admit..." he leaves a trail of soft kisses from my shoulder to my neck. "I could get used to this."

Craig rests his head against mine, placing his hands on my modest bump. He gasps and nudges forward, I instantly register that this time it was not just fluttering. His mouth kicks out into a proud grin. "The baby just kicked!"

"I know, kind of hard for me to miss that one."

"They did it again!"

This is such a surreal feeling. Our baby kicking for the first time. "Oomph! That was a big one."

Craig is insistent on using the body wash on me—or more accurately, my bump. I'm sure he thinks that if he rubs it enough the baby will kick again. No such luck. They've tired themselves out.

After we get out of the bath, he decides to grab my moisturiser and go nuts, again, hoping to feel the baby kick.

He eventually gives up, retreats downstairs, and comes up with the chocolate cake.

"One spoon?" I cock an eyebrow.

"Why not?" he dips the spoon into the cake and points it at my mouth. "Not like we haven't swapped saliva before," he offers me a wolfish grin.

"You're a regular Casanova." I lean forward and wrap my lips around the spoon, my eyes flick up, and notice Craig is watching me intently.

"You love it," he winks, dips the spoon into the cake, then pops the spoon in his mouth.

"I tolerate it."

"Tolerate me, too?"

"Just about."

He narrows his eyes, I try not to laugh but fail miserably.

Craig stares into my eyes, stroking my cheek softly. "I really love you. More than you know."

Hot tears prick my eyes. Soon they are trickling down my cheek. Damn him for making me cry! I can't with these hormones!

"Was it something I said?" he teases.

I sniff, and wipe my tears away, "I love you, too. So much."

"More than cake?"

"I wouldn't go that far."

We finish the cake and go to bed. With my heartburn being so bad, I have to sleep propped up on four pillows.

Craig falls asleep with his head resting just above my bump. Wrapping my arms around him, I run my fingers through his hair until I fall asleep.

CRAIG

$\mathcal{P}$icking out baby names with Lottie is the worst decision I've made so far.

"Theodore?" I suggest.

"Bundy," Lottie claps back without batting an eyelid.

"Freddie?"

"West."

"Jeffrey?"

"Dahmer," her fingers continue tapping away on her keyboard. It's like she's on autopilot mode. I'll never know how women do that.

"James?"

"As in Jim or Jimmy?" she asks, looking up from the screen.

Finally, we are getting somewhere! "Yeah."

"Savile."

"For fuck's sake, Lottie!"

"It's not my fault you have terrible taste in names."

"Aileen for a girl?"

"Wuornos," her eyes flit back to the screen.

"Jane?"

"Toppen."

"Amelia?"

"Dyer."

"There is just no pleasing you, is there?"

"Stop picking the names of serial killers and sex offenders and maybe I'll pick one! What about Ethan?"

"Ethan?"

"Yeah."

"Ethan Barnes... yeah that could work."

"Oh? So we are just sticking your name on the birth

cert?" challenge sparks in her eyes.

"With your fascination with serial killers, yeah, we are going with my name."

"Ellie for a girl?"

My heart skips a beat, "as in Eleanor?"

"Yeah."

I don't know what to say. I'm speechless. Naming the baby after my mom would be amazing, and for Lottie to suggest it, "I..."

"Are you ok?"

"I... Ellie..." I manage to crack a smile through the shock. Damn, it's supposed to be Lottie getting emotional, not me!

"Is that a yes?"

"Yeah, I... love you..."

"You had better," she says with extra sass.

"Way to ruin the moment." She is lucky I'm not into BDSM like Jay or she would be right over my knee. Although—

"I'm tired, cranky, and hungry."

"Is that all?" Hmm, Lottie over my knee... interesting.

"No... kinda horny too."

"So a nap or food first?"

"Mmm food... you know what sounds good..."

"I'm leaving the house for takeout, aren't I?"

"Yeah, you are. Eddie Rockets, my usual. Don't forget the chocolate malt or I won't let you back in the house."

"Yes, boss." I reach over, putting my hand on her face. Pulling her closer, I kiss her forcefully. Lottie sinks into the kiss, her arms wrapping around me, pulling me closer.

"Anything else?" I purr.

"You. Drop your pants." she snags my lower lip between her teeth and my cock practically jumps.

"Excuse me?" That's it. That ass is getting it.

She does not ask again. The next thing I know, Lottie is undoing the button on my pants and yanking the zip down. She works my pants down until they pool at my feet. She reaches down, grasping me, then lowers her head.

I watch as she licks the length of my cock making me shudder, she then kisses the tip before taking the full length in her mouth and tightens her lips, sucking hard, drawing out a moan.

My hands tangle in her hair. "God, yes!" she starts to hum around my length, pushing it to the back of her throat.

"A little harder, baby," she does so immediately continuing to run her mouth from base to tip. "Just like that, baby."

I notice her sliding a hand between her legs as she continues to work me. She's so fucking hot. "Wait, stop, stop!"

Lottie pulls away, pouting. "You don't like this?"

"I love it, baby, but my girl needs attention, too. Come here."

Lottie straddles me, her hands around my neck, I slide my hands down to her waist and pull her against me. Her lips meet mine, teasing my tongue with hers. Lottie can feel how hard I am beneath her, she starts to grind against me, searching for some friction. I kiss her neck, push up the fabric of her skirt and shove those lace panties aside. I slip a finger inside, then another.

Lottie grinds against my hand moaning. I speed up my movements, paying close attention to her clit. Lottie squeezes her eyes shut, grinding against me.

Our sex life is epic. Lottie seems to know what I want on instinct. I've no complaints, none. Though, in truth, there is something we haven't done yet. Something I've been wanting to try. With how eager she is being lately I think she might just agree.

I slide my slick fingers to her ass, Lottie's eyes shoot open. "I really wanna claim this," I admit, kneading that delectable derriere.

"I've never," she gulps.

"Can we try?" I'm all too prepared for her to shoot me down, which is fine. I would never ask her to do anything she was not comfortable with.

"You're huge," she protests. Not a straight-out rejection, hmm... maybe she is curious?

"I'll be gentle."

* * *

I don't know what I've just agreed to, but I trust him. I know as soon as I say stop, he will.

Craig pulls off his shirt and gets to his feet, he looks elated. I turn around and wait for what's to come. Craig gently coaxes my legs apart finding my clit again, he rubs it between his fingers teasing me into a frenzy. I clutch the side cushions on the couch as he continues to tease me closer to the edge of climax.

I then feel his hands move to my rear, "is this, ok?" he slowly dips a slick finger inside ever-so-slightly.

"Yes," my body relaxes to his touch.

Craig slowly pushes his finger in all the way, I gasp, surprised by how good it feels. "Is this, ok?" he asks again, dropping his lips to my shoulder.

"Yes," I confirm.

He finds my clit again, massaging me while he slowly works a second finger into me. I'm throbbing with desire Craig withdraws his hands and I feel him rub the head of his length between my wet folds.

"Are you ready?"

"I think so."

He presses inside me, thrusting slowly. He slides his fingers back to my clit, moving them in time with thrusts.

My heart is pounding with anticipation, he presses the tip into me and I grip the cushions tighter, "Craig, you're too big."

"Do you want me to stop?" his hips don't move. He shifts to look at me.

"I don't know."

"Lottie," his lips brush my shoulder, "do you want me to stop?" There is no disappointment or anger in his tone.

"N-no."

"Are you sure?"

I give him a nod then claw at the cushions, ready for him to continue.

Craig's deft fingers find that bundle of nerves again, and he starts to rub himself between my folds, then claims me once again. He presses one delicious inch at a time until he's all the way inside.

"Is this, ok?"

"Y-yes!"

Slowly he withdraws then presses back in, and I cry out. His strokes are slow, deliberate. Pretty soon they start to feel unbelievably good.

Craig continues to rub me as he slowly pumps into me, that beautiful man bringing me closer. I push myself up on my knees and feel his python-like grip securing me. His lips find mine, muffling his approving growls.

I slide my arm around his neck, playing with the tufts of his hair, Craig slides a hand between my legs and I'm certain I'm about to blackout.

My legs begin to tremble. Ache and ecstasy melt together.

"Lottie, fuck— baby—I can't hold out," the words barely

register, I'm flooded with an earth-shattering orgasm. I feel Craig tense behind me at the same time, he grips me hard enough to leave marks. His breath brushing the back of my neck, he cusses, kissing my neck and shoulder, then pulls out. I turn to face him and he draws a line from my cheekbone to my mouth with his thumb. His tender lips meet mine. "Are you ok, baby?"

"I'm fine," I grin up at him.

"Hungry?" he nuzzles into my neck.

"Famished."

"I'll go to Eddie's and get us some food. I won't be long."

* * *

I go upstairs, Craig follows. Setting up Netflix, he insists that I go and rest in bed before he leaves. I love how protective he is of us. Of how safe he makes me feel. Oh how doting he is, Craig surprises me with flowers and chocolates and gifts because he wants to, not because he is trying to win me over because he was a dick like Michael used to do.

Michael would push and push me, and when I finally had enough and left, he would go out of his way to apologise, to win me back, and like the fool I am, I kept falling for it.

Craig is so vastly different, he constantly wants to hold me, to be near me, to love me in a way no one ever has. I can understand that now because all I want is to be with Craig, not for his money, or his connections, but to just have him. I still can't believe that I have him, he's mine. We are having a baby together. I feel like I've won the lottery.

After about fifteen minutes I hear a knock on the door. He must have his hands full, normally he would just let himself in.

"You better have my malt, Barnes, or I—" I gawk at the person on the other side of the door. "Michael?"

"Hi, Char."

"What are you doing here?" I demand, folding my arms across my chest.

"I need to speak with you. Can we talk?"

"It's not a good time, Craig will be home soon—"

"He is what I wanted to talk to you about."

LOTTIE

"*W*hat do you mean?"

"Can I come in? I promise I won't be long."

"How did you know where I live?" I don't move from the doorway. I don't want him in my house. It's like inviting a vampire in. I wonder if I chucked some garlic at him would he run?

"I... followed Craig here after the gym," he admits.

"YOU WHAT?"

"It's not as bad as it sounds, I swear!"

"You're stalking my boyfriend!" feck the garlic, I'll take the stake.

"No, I mean—not like that. I needed to see you. To warn you—"

"Warn me about what?"

"He's cheating on you, Char."

I blink in shock. *He fucking what now?* Stepping aside unconsciously I allow Michael to come inside. "Pot calling the kettle black?"

"I know, I know I was an idiot. I fucked up. What I did was unforgivable. I know that. I'm sorry."

"This is a mistake, you shouldn't be here. I think you should leave."

"Char, look... given your..." his eyes fall to my bump. "Condition, I had to tell you. He is working at my girlfriend's house. I thought she was acting weird so I checked out her phone. No texts, obviously, but there are numerous calls to his number."

"That's work-related. It's not uncommon for Craig to speak with clients regularly."

"That's what I thought at first, but then she start... I

don't know... acting weird."

"Weird how?"

"She would get a call and leave the room, try to hide who was calling her by turning the phone away. If I asked about it, she start saying it was her mom or one of her friends, it didn't add up to parts of the conversations I overheard.

"Like what?"

"Like flirting and shit. Pot calling the kettle black as you say. I deserve it after what I did to you, but you don't deserve another unfaithful lover. Not when you have that child on the way." Michael looks sincere, his eyes pleading with me to believe him. "I may have been a pig, but I would never have done that to you if you were carrying my child."

"Craig would never—"

"I confronted him at the gym a few weeks ago. That's why I was there. He lost it, threatened me."

"I don't believe you."

"I reported it to the garda."

"Nick would have said something."

"Nick probably made it go away. I haven't heard a thing since. Once my name was mentioned that was that, you know how much he hates me."

I scoff, this is getting ridiculous now. He is getting ridiculous now! "Nick would never cover up a crime!" My hands slam on my hips.

"Maybe he thought I was bullshitting him? I don't know. Come on, Char, you're telling me that you haven't noticed anything suspicious, at all? No weird phone calls or excuses that don't add up?" Michael paces then stops in front of the door so I cannot fling him out.

"No," there is no way. Craig would never do that to me. He wouldn't— there were those phone calls now that I think of it, and that weird number... "Was it you?"

"Was what me?"

"Those creepy texts, the pictures?"

"I've no idea what you're talking about."

"Come on, Michael. You just admitted to following Craig to find out where I live!"

"To warn you to get away from him!"

A warning to stay away from Craig, it had to be him!

"Look, believe me, or don't, I came to you with what I know, my conscience is clear," Michael spins for the door. As he opens it, Craig's van pulls up.

"What the hell are you doing here?" Craig's out of the van and charging at Michael.

"Filling Char in on our little talk at the gym a few weeks ago."

Craig's eyes find mine for a split second then jump back to Michael. "I told you to stay the hell away from her."

"Afraid that I'll let the cat out of the bag? You've been lying to her! Deceiving her for weeks!"

"You shut your fucking mouth!" Craig's countenance is unnerving to behold, something dangerous sparks behind his eyes. I have never seen him this annoyed.

"Craig?"

"Go inside, Lottie. I'll be there in a minute."

"Yeah, he doesn't want you to hear what kind of man you're dating."

Craig steps up, looking like he is about ready to strike Michael.

"Go ahead! Make sure you leave a nice big bruise. Assault charges with evidence that even Nick can't cover up for you!"

"Leave, Michael," I demand. I am not having a fistfight breaking out in my front garden, I am not having Craig arrested and imprisoned before this baby is born.

* * *

The bastard nods to Lottie then turns in my direction and smirks. "I warned you to stay away from her," he mumbles lowly as he walks by me.

I pull out my phone immediately.

"Who are you calling?" Lottie asks hesitantly.

"Nick."

Voicemail. Dammit!

"Go on inside," turning back to the van, I pull out the food and follow Lottie into the house.

"Is it true?" Lottie demands as soon as the door clicks shut.

"Is what true?"

"The gym incident. He reported you to the gards?"

I sigh. I didn't want her involved in this shit. I don't want her to stress while she's pregnant. "Yes. It's true."

"And you didn't tell me!"

"I didn't want you to worry."

"What did you say to him?"

"I know he was behind those messages you were getting, those threats. When he showed up at the gym out of the blue, I knew he was following us. I pulled him aside and told him to quit while he was ahead. No more messages or scare tactics. He didn't like what I had to say so the little shit went and reported me."

"You should have told me!"

"I know. I'm sorry, I just— I thought I was doing the right thing, protecting you and our baby. You were so anxious when those texts started, I didn't want you to go through it again."

"That's it then? That's everything I should know?"

"Yes. I didn't do anything to him, I swear—tempted as I was."

"And you're working on his girlfriend's house?"

"Am I?" That's news to me. We have five contracts at the moment.

"Apparently so."

"Someone should tell the poor girl to run for the hills. Do you know a name?" As soon as I ask the question Lottie instantly relaxes as if my lack of knowledge about this girl is a good thing.

"No, I never caught it."

"I've two women that I'm working for, the other three are men. If I had to venture a guess, I'd say Linda, she is closer to our age," I step in from the hallway and make my way to the kitchen. "The house is a nightmare."

"Nightmare, how?"

I grab two plates from the presses and start serving up the food. "Built by cowboys. Dylan's doing his nut in, he had to tear out all the pipes in the kitchen and put new ones in. They were all angled wrong or something. All the food was getting caught in them and the kitchen constantly stunk."

"That bad?"

"Worse. Dylan and Jay are still working on it. The only thing I need to do is go back in once Jay is done rewiring the kitchen and put new floors upstairs."

I bring the food into the sitting room and offer Lottie her chocolate malt. I have got the right mind to get back in the van and go after Michael, but after that run-in, Lottie will need me here. "Did he say anything else to you?"

"No, nothing," she shakes her head and takes a sip of her malt.

"You ok, baby?"

"Tired," she gifts me a weak smile.

"Well, let's head upstairs then and have this in bed, yeah?"

"Yeah, that sounds nice."

Nick rings me a little while later. "Took your time!"

"What's up?" he asks, sounding a little bored.

"Michael showed up at the house."

"He what?"

"I went out to get dinner. I wasn't gone long, like twenty minutes maybe? When I got back, he was in the house."

"Break in?"

I sigh, "sadly not. Lottie let him in. He's been following us. I told you he is the same bastard that's responsible for the pictures."

"Why did Lottie let him in?"

"I blame the hormones," I lean back against the headboard.

"They clouded my judgement," Lottie calls over a mouthful of cheese fries.

"What did he want?" Nick demands.

"To warn Lottie away from me apparently. He mentioned the incident at the gym."

"Why would he do that?"

"Probably hoping that I would deny it and look like I had something to hide? I don't know."

"He followed Craig home," Lottie announces, then casually takes a sip of her malt.

"He what!" Nick's voice booms over the phone.

I look at Lottie who shrugs in response. Too preoccupied with her food to care that she failed to mention that earlier.

"We have to have something on that right? Like stalking or some shit?" I say to Nick.

"No proof," Nick sighs.

"He admitted it."

"It's all hearsay. He could just as easily deny everything

if questioned."

"But he knows where we live!"

I was your roommate remember? I used to live there. My sister is pregnant with your child, he could just say that he didn't know she was there and chanced it, hoping she did live with you or was at least in the house at the time of him calling."

"There is footage of him at the house!"

"You said Lottie let him in."

"For fuck's sake!" I toss my feet up on the bed, almost knocking over my plate.

"I know, I know it's infuriating but legally speaking you have nothing to go on. He's a devious bastard but he's smart. You didn't punch him, did you?"

"I bloody wish I had now!"

"Put Lottie on the phone..."

Lottie takes another mouthful of malt then takes the phone. "What do you want?"

"You let him in!"

"Don't yell at the pregnant woman."

"What the hell, Lottie? You should know better!"

"Obviously not, baby brain and all that jazz."

"I can't believe you would be so stupid!"

"Don't you go taking that tone with me, you limp noodle!"

We really should not have watched Mulan before taking this call.

"Do I have to come over there?"

"And what are you going to do, Nick? Spank me?"

"Babe! That's just wrong on so many levels."

"Shut up you, you filthy little beast," she growls at me.

I steal a forkful of her fries while she's distracted by Nick's tantrum.

"You need to think before you act, Lottie!" Nick growls.

"Oh, I'm thinking, alright. I'm thinking of hanging up the phone and shagging your best friend on spite!"

"Leave me out of this!" I almost choke on a cheese chip.

"That's not what you said on the couch," she claps back.

"Touche."

"For fuck's sake!" Nick grumbles.

Lottie grins victoriously and hands me back the phone. Nick hung up, obviously too uncomfortable with the thoughts of his sister violating me.

Her phone rings soon after. Lottie doesn't check the screen. "Back so soon? Good, tell me, what's the best lube to use for anal?"

"Charlotte Evans!" Kim's voice bellows over the phone.

"Oh, hi mom..." she blushes to her roots.

I'm doubled up on the bed, laughing my ass off.

"I thought you were Nick!" she squeals.

"Yeah, that's not sounding much better, babe." Lottie kicks me and scrambles from the bed. I can hear parts of her conversation with Kim as she walks downstairs.

My phone vibrates somewhere on the bed. I toss over blankets and napkins before I find it. "Jay?"

"I need to come over and borrow that saw again."

"Yeah sure." Another small fortune went on the replacement.

Mom for goodness sake, it was a joke! Lottie's voice floats upstairs. *Anal isn't that bad! I could have said much worse!*

"Am I missing something here?" Jay asks.

"I'll explain when I see you," I grab another cheese chip.

Like eating a carrot from a nun's snatch!

"Aaaand that's my cue to go."

"Good call," I hang up just as Lottie stomps her way back upstairs.

"I don't even want to know..."

"Shut up, Mr. Asphyxiation wank in a batman suit!"

"Why am I to blame?" I can't help but laugh at her, she's so cute when she's in a strop.

"You say shit like that and it's funny. I say it and it's offensive!"

"Kim wasn't impressed?"

"She'll find it funny eventually."

My phone rings again, I reach over to answer while Lottie is still ranting.

"Like it was a lube joke for fuck's sake, lube!" Lottie gesticulates wildly.

"Hello?"

"There is a lube I found online called whisky dick, I think Lottie might like it."

"Josie!" Kill me now.

"What? She said lube, right?"

"I did, Josephine!" Lottie shouts victoriously.

"Don't encourage her!" I warn, turning to Lottie who gives me an impish grin in response.

"Lottie is very young to be needing that though, no? Oh, unless it's for up the bum?"

"Nan!!!"

Lottie is hanging onto the bed, her face buried into the blanket. To say she is howling with laughter would be a gross understatement.

"Dinner tomorrow night?" Josie asks, like she hasn't just traumatised me for life.

"Yeah."

"Good, see you then!"

"Why is this family so fucking dysfunctional?" I ask, hanging up the phone.

Screw it!

Lottie can't answer me, tears are free-flowing down her face as she continues to laugh and snort into the blanket. Only stopping to come up for air.

CRAIG

"*H*ow are the nipples, Lottie?"

"Nan!"

"What? It's a valid question," Josie's voice rasps, completely unaware of how abnormal this question is.

"They're good thanks, still there last I checked," Lottie replies casually.

"Any leaking?"

"Not yet. Mom said she didn't produce milk until like three days after Nick and I were born, so I might be like her."

"I wish I was that lucky. I remember with Eleanor, I thought I was getting lucky. Well, one night Bobby came in from the pub—"

"Don't do it, Josie, don't do it—" I'm begging you!

"Safe to say he got more than a mouthful if you get my drift."

"And she went there."

* * *

Craig gets up and walks out of the room.

"Nothing like that yet, thank God."

"And how has Craig been?"

"Great. Very attentive with everything. He's excited about the baby coming."

"He will be a great father. Though, I hope he is not neglecting you with all of this baby excitement."

"Not at all, he is spoiling me rotten."

"And tending to your needs, I hope..."

"I left the room for two minutes!" Craig groans from the

doorway.

"Oh, calm down and stop being such a drama queen. Sex is natural. You wouldn't be here without it, so pipe down."

"I am not discussing our sex life with you," he moans.

"Well, that's why I asked Lottie."

"She is quite satisfied, thanks," Craig chimes in from the other side of the room. "Now, can we move on, please?"

"I'm only saying that a lot of men neglect their partner when she is expecting. Some are nervous about hurting the baby, others just take some time adapting to the changes—"

"Josie... we are good, drop it!"

"Fine. Fine!"

Craig sits at the table, resting his hand on my knee, he gives a gentle squeeze.

"They had apple tart or rhubarb. I was not sure what to get, so I picked both," George calls from the hallway.

"Brilliant, thank you. Oh, Lottie! George and I took a class the other day. Very educational and quite enjoyable. I think you would like it."

"What class was that?"

"Tantric massage," Josie's eyes twinkle impishly.

Craig chokes on his drink. Spittle flies across the table. He stands, still choking, and flees the room.

"I don't think he's coming back," I stare at the doorway, Craig just ran out.

It takes a good twenty minutes for Craig to return. I help Josie tidy up after we have eaten and she insists on pulling out the photo albums for the millionth time since Craig and I got together.

I must admit, Craig is every bit his mother. There is hardly a trace of his father in his face. Something Craig takes pride in.

He was a mamma's boy. In almost every picture, he is in her arms or by her side.

My phone rings and I excuse myself to take the call.

"Hello?"

"Hey, girl!"

"Tiffy, what's up?"

"I'm bored, thinking of coming over early if you're in?" I hear the clank of dishes in the background.

"In Josie's right now but we should be back in about an hour or so."

"Ah right. Oh, by the way, what are you doing two weeks from Friday?" Cupboard doors bang shut and I can only assume that she is emptying the dishwasher.

"Nothing, why?"

"Wrong! Spa weekend."

"I'm too fat for a spa weekend."

"First of all, you are not fat, you're pregnant! Secondly, shut up. It's your baby shower."

"Really?"

"Yep. I've arranged everything and paid for it all."

The joys of your best friend being loaded. Well, her daddy being loaded and her being his only daughter.

"Does my mom know?"

"Yep, why?"

"She's kind of pissed at me. Poorly timed anal joke. I'll explain when I see you."

"When was the last time your mom was with a guy?"

"I don't want to know."

"I'm just saying, maybe she could use a thumb up the butt or something. It might take the edge off."

"Thanks for that," I throw my eyes to the heavens.

"Any time!"

"I better go back in and save Craig."

"Josephine being as colourful as always?"

"She brought up tantric massage..."

"Stop!" Tiffy cackles down the phone. "I'm sure he loved that."

"Who Craig or George?"

Another booming laugh from Tiffy. "Fair play to her. I hope I still have good sex when I get to her age."

"Yeah, she's living the dream."

"Ok, I'll let you go and see you around... eight... give you some time to get back and for Craig to wash away his trauma."

"Sounds good!"

* * *

I couldn't get out of Josie's quick enough. The woman thinks now that she has a new... whatever George is, that it's ok to mention sex to me.

I forgot that it's the first Friday of the month. A tradition for Lottie and Tiffy to have a sleepover. So I'll be listening to endless out-of-tune singing and playing snack bitch for the night.

I used to use these nights to go out with the lads, or just go on the pull. For the last few months, I seem to be Lottie's personal manservant.

Ben and Jerry's, stuffed crust pizzas, cookies, and I get nothing. I tried to sneak a cookie last month, Lottie caught me and almost throat punched me for it.

"What's Jay doing?"

"Probably playing the Xbox," Tiffy responds. The girls are dressed in animal onesies. Lottie is a rabbit, ears on the hood and all, and Tiffy is a cow. They're like a pair of oversized toddlers.

"Ooh, Mama Mia!" Lottie chirps.

"Bollocks off, I'm out—enjoy!" Grabbing the keys to the

van, I run out the door. I try ringing Jay but there is no
answer. So I try Nick.

"Hello?"

"Tell me you're not working!"

"Sleepover night..."

"Wouldn't you know!"

"Nah, I'm off tonight, Jay is here if you want to come
over."

"On the way!"

Beer pong at our age. I've concluded that drinking past the
age of twenty-five is fucking lethal! Or it could be the fact
that we ran out of beer after an hour and instead, cracked
open the JD.

"Yes, swallow it!" I demand.

Jay laughs, spitting out some of the whisky.

"Lightweight!" Nick teases.

"Suck my dick!" Jay wipes his mouth on his sleeve.

"I'd need tweezers and a magnifying glass to find it
first," Nick snorts.

I check my phone while the pair trade insults. I'm
seeing double.

Lottie

Hey babe, will you be home soon? xxx

I check the time. Two in the morning, she sent that at half
twelve... shit. I can't see straight enough to text so I ring her
instead.

"Hey, where are you?"

"Sorry, baby. I'm at Nick's with Jay."

"Are you drunk?" I can hear 80's music shuffling about
in the background. Clearly, Tiffy is looking for a song to

blast.

"Eh, define drunk?"

"You're sloshed."

"I'm not slished."

"You're definitely sloshed," she chuckles and I can't help but smile at the sound.

"Am not."

"Whatever you say, batman."

"What are you wearing?" I mumble, taking a few long strides away from the lads.

"Hey!" Nick snaps.

"Shhhh, you'll wake Abbie!" I dismiss him instantly.

"That's my sister!"

"Abbie's your wife, dumbass!"

"No, I mean—"

"Oooh, boobies!" I turn to see Jay staring intently at his phone.

"Tell Tiffy to put those baps away," I snort, hearing Lottie giggle.

"Tell her to take it off!" Jay demands.

"You're staying in Nick's tonight then?" Lottie asks.

"Yip."

"Ok. I'll see you tomorrow. Love you."

"Liv you too, baby!" I hang up just as Jay takes his shot.

"Ha! Drink it!"

"Ah, cum guzzler!

* * *

The guys have updated their Instagram stories throughout the night. Getting more and more pissed as the night went on.

"They'll be feeling that today," Tiffy mumbles, rolling on her side to face me, she snuggles into her pillow, unwilling to move.

As if summoned by the mere mention of their names, the key turns in the front door and two sets of footsteps climb the stairs.

"Never again," Craig groans. The bedroom door opens and he falls on the side of the bed beside me.

"Kill me now," Jay mirrors Craig's actions and falls beside Tiffy.

"Self-inflicted," I tease. Craig groans and pulls me in closer to him, burying his head in my back.

"How did you get here? Neither of you are in any shape to drive," Tiffy asks.

"Taxi," Jay stifles a yawn.

"What about the van?"

"We'll get it eventually when we're not dying of the plague," Jay grunts.

"Men! You're so dramatic," I feel Craig's hold tighten on me. He stays silent, feeling too sorry for himself to attempt to defend his drinking.

"You're hungover, get over it!" Tiffy scoffs.

"Never!" Jay protests.

"Want a belly rub?"

"Do you want me to teabag you?"

"Not in this fucking bed you won't!" Craig barks.

"It looks like an orgy in here," I smirk, looking at the four of us crammed into the bed.

"A snuggle orgy," Tiffy whips out her phone, holding it high in the air. "Everybody say struggle cuddle!" She snaps the picture and smiles triumphantly. "Now that's a good-looking foursome."

"I mean, me and you clearly make that picture. The other two are just props," I hiss, feeling Craig's teeth scrape my shoulder.

"Obviously," Tiffy finishes adding in her hashtags under the picture and clicks post.

"I feel so cheap," Jay feigns outrage.

"You smell it, too," Tiffy crinkles her nose.

"See the abuse I put up with!"

"Lottie's worse," Craig sniggers.

"Screw you, too!"

"Which hole?" I elbow him in the ribs and he doubles over, laughing. "Battered husband syndrome!"

"We aren't married."

"Battered man friend syndrome..."

"Better."

"Kiss it better."

"Nah, you stink."

"If only I had an ego, it would be bruised right now."

"Who took that boobalicious picture of you last night?" Jay asks Tiffy.

"Me, obviously!" Jay looks at me with an unreadable expression on his face. "You photographed her naked?"

"Yeah, and?"

"Not like she hasn't seen me before," Tiffy shrugs.

"What else do you do?" Jay props himself up eagerly.

"Oh, you know... lingerie pillow fights, kissing—"

"Scissoring and general foreplay," Tiffy adds.

"Don't forget the sex toys."

"How could I forget," she gives me a wolfish smile.

"I know you two are winding me up right now, but I'm keeping that image for my wank bank."

"Get the image of my Mrs out of your head!" Craig snaps.

"Too late, she's in there with Josie."

"WHAT?" Craig shoots up in the bed.

"Total GILF."

There is a cacophony of laughter from the girls.

"You two have serious issues," Tiffy sighs.

"Keep it up and your mam is next," Jay warns.

"You'll have to lure her out of the pub with a pint."

"Are we invited to this baby shower?" Craig asks, changing the subject.

"No," Tiffy doesn't look up from her phone.

"Why?"

"For women only."

"But it's my baby!"

"Ask my tits."

"We'll wet the baby's head while they're away," Jay declares.

"Not a hope. I think I've got liver damage already," Craig's head drops back to the pillow.

"Sleepover?" Jay presses.

"Only if I get to be the big spoon."

"Better buy me dinner first."

"I'll bring the lube."

"Vaseline not Vaporub or you'll have a lightsabre," Jay grins.

"And you'll have serious ring sting."

"Should we leave you two alone?" Tiffy asks.

"I think we should," I attempt to move but Craig pins me to the bed.

"You move this arse so much as an inch from me and I'll tie you to the bed."

"Intriguing... tell me more."

"Please do, my bank is running low." Craig swings a pillow at Jay's head.

"How do you put up with him?" I ask Tiffy.

"He's pretty."

"Thanks, babe."

"So... snuggle orgy day?" Tiffy asks.

"Pretty much," we all shrug and recline against the

cushions.

"Say hangover!" Tiffy raises the phone high in the air again to snap another picture.

LOTTIE

"Curse you tiny toilet!"

"You've been watching the minions again, haven't you?" Shannon asks.

"Little bit," I nod even though she cannot see me over the phone. "Die, Morgan Freeman, you son of a bitch!"

"Playing SouthPark again?"

"Yep."

"Stick of truth?"

"The fractured but whole. Oh my god, they killed Kenny!"

"You bastards!"

"This is why we're friends!"

"Speaking of fractured butt holes, if you're given the choice to cut or tear, choose cut. Carter destroyed me, it was like a black hole down there. I'm sure there was an echo coming through at one stage before I was stitched back together."

"What a way to put me at ease about the birth, thanks for that!"

"Any time. When is the big scan again?"

"Tomorrow."

"You guys finding out what you're having?"

"No. I think I want to keep it a surprise. As long as the baby is healthy, I could care less what sex they are."

"And you and Craig, you're good, right? I mean, after the whole Michael thing..."

"Yeah, we're good."

"Did he hit the roof about the cheating accusation?"

"I didn't actually tell him about it. I was going to but, I mean, what's the point? To be honest, Michael did get in my head a bit. I'll admit I start questioning it once the weird phone calls thing was mentioned..."

"Lottie, please! Craig has been in love with you since he met you. Any idiot could see it. Plus, let's face it. It's Craig. He is not exactly one to beat around the bush. You know where you stand with him, there is never any pussyfooting about."

"I know. I do. As soon as I hinted at Michael's girlfriend, I could see the confusion on Craig's face. He genuinely didn't know who I was talking about at first until he started trying to add it up."

"He would never do anything to hurt you. He was never the cheating kind anyway, you've seen him. He was never shy about telling girls that he was not into them or it wasn't going anywhere. He is the type to just be blunt."

"Yeah, you're right. I know you're right. I know Craig. I still cannot fully explain those weird phone calls but he wouldn't hurt me and definitely wouldn't do anything on our baby. After his dad walking out on him, it's his life's mission to do the complete opposite. If anything, he is going to be a helicopter parent.

"Can you imagine if it is a girl?"

"I'll have to apologise in advance because the poor girl will never be allowed out of his sights."

"Imagine her going to a sleepover, he would probably pack himself a sleeping bag and join in!"

"I would not be the slightest bit surprised." My phone beeps and I check the screen. "Shit, I gotta go, my mom's calling."

"K, bye!"

I take a deep breath in to steady myself then answer the phone. "Hello?"

"Now that is the way you answer the phone."

"Oh, give it a rest."

"Is that any way to talk to your mother?"

"I'm up half the night with heartburn, the other half with Craig's snoring. I bit into an apple and puked it back up. I'm constipated and cranky. So, yes. That is exactly how I'm going to talk to you."

"I heard Michael was around..."

"He's like a fucking yeast infection."

"Lovely analogy."

"I think so."

"What did he want?"

"He tried to say Craig is cheating on me with his girlfriend."

"Urgh, tell him to grip his ears tightly and pull his head out of his ass!"

"Oh, so it's ok for you to make ass jokes!"

"Our boy would never do that to you." I love the way she completely blanks my statement. *Our boy,* as in Craig. It is no surprise at all that mom has always had a sweet spot for him. Now that we are officially together, she has started calling him her son-in-law. I keep telling her that we need to be married for her to use that title but she won't hear of it. That's her boy now.

"I know mom."

"I hope Craig sorted him out."

"That would be assault and he could get arrested."

"I would love to smack the smug smirk off that little prick's face after what he did to you."

"I'm glad he cheated. If he didn't then I wouldn't be here now."

"True. Craig is the best thing to happen to you. You smile more since being with him."

"True. He is. I do."

"About time you got yourself a real man."

"Yeah, because those blow-up dolls just weren't cutting

it anymore."

"I see somebody is in a snarky mood today."

"Maybe if I could poop I would feel better."

"Where is my favourite son-in-law?"

Only son-in-law, if we were married. "Work, as always."

"We should do a barbecue. A family one to celebrate the baby!"

"Which translates into you're going to make Craig play chef while you get busy making cocktails."

"He knows how to work a grill!"

* * *

Four years earlier

Nick is in the middle of getting a bollocking off mom for God only knows what. Golden boy in trouble. It's usually me. I glance up and spot Craig chugging his beer and sniggering, then he proceeds to flip the burgers on the grill.

"Smells good!" Tiffy drops in the seat next to me.

"It does," I nod, trying to read my odd sisters' book but the sight of a shirtless Craig inches from me with beads of sweat rolling down his chest is... well... distracting. Why does he have to look so damn good?

His latest conquest is over flirting with Jason, neither Tiffy nor Craig seem in any way bothered by it. She is attractive I'll give her that. Box dyed red hair, large brown eyes, curvy. The sad thing is she's actually nice. I can't find a reason to dislike her other than I just don't want her with Craig.

I don't know why I'm even thinking like that. I mean, I have Michael... where ever he is. He's floating about here somewhere. Craig is just my brother's hot as hell roommate. Men like him don't look at girls like me. It's just fact.

"Charlotte!" My head instantly springs up, Craig smiles at me, shaking an empty bottle in the air. "Do you mind getting me another one? If I go searching I'll burn these."

"Sure," I place my book down and go get the empty bottle so I know what brand to get him. "You know Nick should be the one on the grill, you're a guest here."

"I don't mind."

"Jenny seems nice," Craig follows my gaze, his eyebrows shooting to his hairline before he shakes his head and smirks, almost like he forgot she was even there.

"Yeah. She's a nice girl."

I excuse myself and go inside to top Craig up. When I come back out, Jay and Tiffy are gone. Snuck off for a quicky most likely, Nick is now talking to Jenny and Mom has pushed by me to make some sangria.

"Thanks, doll," Craig takes the bottle off me and chugs. "Where is Matthew?"

"Matthew?" My brow furrows for a moment before I realise who he is talking about. "Oh! Do you mean Michael? Erm... I'm not too sure actually."

"You two together long?"

"A few months now."

"And he is already abandoning you at family events?"

"I'm sure he's just on a work call."

Craig is suddenly enchanted by the barbecue, the playful smile on his face vanishing. "How do you like it?"

"Huh?" I blush to my roots, turning to him I spot a playful glint in his eye.

"Your burger, doll?" he smirks.

"Oh! Erm, whatever, I'm easy..." Oh my God! Now I'm the town bike. Kill me now!

He serves up ours first since everyone else seems to have vanished, then pops some more meat patties on the grill.

I bite into the burger, moaning, "this is really good!"

He chuckles, I notice him staring at my lip.

"You've... umm..." he reaches out brushing away a blob of sauce from the corner of my mouth.

"Oh," why am I such an awkward mess?

"I'm glad you like it," his tone is soft, low, sweet.

"Oh good, I'm starving!" Michael appears in the garden, marching straight for the table.

"Where were you?" I ask, reluctantly pulling my gaze from Craig.

"Huh? Oh, inside on a call," he reaches for the plate of burgers, then his eyes fall to me. "No salad?"

"It's on the burger," Craig snorts. He is smiling but there is something else in his face that I can't quite read.

"You might want to ease up on the alcopops and cocktails," Michael cautions before taking a sizeable chunk from his burger. "All those empty calories."

Craig's eyes jump from me to Michael and back again.

Mom comes out with her pitcher and lands in the seat next to Craig, Nick joins us and soon everyone is at the table, digging in.

Jenny is practically sitting on Craig's lip, stroking his arm and laughing at everything he says, be it funny or not. I excuse myself and go inside to grab a hoodie, with the sun going down I'm starting to feel a chill.

"Hey!" Craig's voice follows me down the hall.

"Hey, you ok?"

He quick-walks to me, his hands shoved in his pockets as he approaches. "I know we don't know each other very well, you can tell me to shove it if you want but—"

"Craig, are you alright?"

"Michael... is he— I mean are you... ok? He treats you well?"

"Yeah, he treats me fine, why?"

"Just curious, he seems a bit... off. I just— erm... if he mistreats you— can I see your phone?"

I'm absolutely dumbfounded but find myself handing him my phone anyway. Craig taps away at the screen then his phone chimes and hangs up on the second ring.

"Now you have my number. If you need anything, Charlotte, don't be afraid to ring me, ok?"

"OK. Thank you."

Craig nods then gives me an awkward smile and turns down the hallway.

"Craig!" He stops and turns to look over his shoulder. "Call me Lottie."

* * *

"Charlotte, are you there?" Mom's voice pulls me back to reality.

"You couldn't be arsed doing it yourself," I snort.

"That too! Invite Josephine."

"Mom, if you don't like my talk about anal, you'll hate speaking with Josie now that she has a boyfriend."

"Nonsense. We are all adults."

"Yet you chewed the ear off me for a joke."

"I was having a bad day."

"So the stick slid out of your ass or did you get a much-needed one up there?"

"Lottie!" Her voice screeches on the other side of the phone.

"Blame the baby." I end the call with mom and check the time. I'm bored out of my head, sitting around all day. Craig has done all the housework so I have nothing to do bar sit here and get fat.

Hmm, I could get the bus into town? Do some

shopping?

I check the time, twenty-past-eleven. I could bring Craig some lunch, channel my inner Martha Stewart.

* * *

It's official. I'm going to be done for murder.

Someone is one stupid question away from me going snap happy with the nail gun.

Bollocks to this, bollocks to work, bollocks to everything today!

Everything is going wrong, late deliveries, two lads called in sick and on top of everything, Sarah, the owner of the house is home and won't take the hint to piss off. She is a client so I have to be polite about it but she's testing my last nerve.

"You're so good at what you do, Craig," she attempts to push out the bee stings she calls breasts.

"Thank you."

She twirls her hair around her finger and starts batting her lashes at me. It's not like Sarah is bad-looking exactly, she just looks like she has been blasted with Homer Simpson's makeup gun.

"Would you like some..." she tosses her hair over her shoulder, "refreshments?"

"I'm good, thanks. I'll have to move you so I can get in and measure this."

She sidesteps me and I'm almost certain she is checking out my ass as I bend down to measure the space for the new units.

My phone buzzes on top of my toolbox, I catch Sarah stealing a glance at the screen as I go for it. Nosey bitch.

"Hey, baby!"

Sarah's eyes narrow and she walks away. About damn

time!

"Hey, are you busy?"

"I can make time for you. What's up?"

"You're working on that house in Poppintree, right? The one with the solar panels?"

"Yeah, that's it. Why? Do you need me to come home?"

"No, I'm outside."

"You're what?" Turning for the door, I catch a glimpse of Lottie down by the gate. "I'll be out in a sec." I hang up and walk back into the kitchen. "Dylan, go and get yourself fed. Be back in an hour."

"Great, I'm starving!"

Grabbing my wallet and keys, I hurry outside to meet Lottie. "This is a surprise."

"A good surprise I hope?"

"Definitely."

She is armed with a bag full of food, "hope you're hungry."

"Famished."

"So how is work going?" She asks while I scoff the chicken fillet roll she brought me for lunch.

"A nightmare."

"That good?"

"I wouldn't mind so much, but the owner seems out to poach me."

"I thought you would like the attention?"

"Only from you, baby."

"Which one is she?" Lottie looks towards the gate, Sarah and her two friends are talking in direct view of the van.

"The Oompa Loompa."

"Ah, got it. How about I just take you home with me?"

"Don't tempt me. If two of the guys hadn't called in sick, I would have left already."

"You would be bored all day at home with nothing to do."

"Not true. I'd have you..."

"What else could you possibly surprise me with after anal?"

"I have quite the colourful imagination. I'm sure I could think of something."

"I don't doubt it," Lottie glances out the window and smiles. "Your stalker does not seem impressed by my presence."

"She can shove it up her hole." Sarah continues to glare into the van with her friends. I make a point of pulling Lottie onto my lap, kissing her slowly, deliberately. I don't give a rat's furry ass who sees us. Let them watch.

"Are you seriously tenting already?" Lottie sniggers.

"Can't help it. You have me like a horny teenager."

"You'll be going back to work with a raging hard-on."

"Don't send me back in there like this, I'll feel like the new inmate in the prison shower!"

"Have you ever heard of the term privacy?" She gestures to our surroundings. Sarah and her friends, the neighbours walking by.

"Have you ever heard the term blue-balls?"

"You'll have to survive until you get home tonight."

"Urgh, I hate today. You can't throw me to the wolves, babe. Look at them. They're looking at me like a snack."

"I can't stay here. One, this is her house and I'm sure she would have Mickey-fit. Two, I'm pregnant and that sawdust is not good for me to be breathing in. Stop sulking!"

"No," I practically slump in my seat.

"I'll make it up to you."

"How?"

"I'll let you tie me up and have your way with me," I raise an eyebrow at him and bite my lower lip.

"If you're joking that's just mean."

"No jokes."

"None?"

"Nope."

"So if I wanted to... tie you up and use your toys on you?"

"You could do it," she offers me a sweet smile.

"What if I wanted to claim this fine ass again?" wow, I could fry an egg on her face right now, she's blushing to her roots.

"You could do it,"

My cock jumps at the thought. I know some girls have pet names for their guy's... friend. I put a stop to that once Jenny start calling him Mr. Winky. Nothing turns a guy flaccid than a name like that. Although, Lottie talking about her ex's shrivelled up meat wand came close. I felt sorry for the guy. Not enough to stop me laughing my ass off.

"What if I just wanted to feast on that sweet pussy for the night?"

"There is really nothing I could do to stop you, now is there? My hands would be tied." She looks up at me through lowered lashes and it takes every ounce of self-control not to drive off with her right now.

"Why are you such a tease?"

"You love me."

"I'd love to put you over my knee right now, but I have to go back in."

Lottie leans in, our lips fusing together.

Drive. Just leave. They won't even notice you're gone!

"I'll see you later tonight."

Noooooooooo, take me with you!!!!

"If I don't show up. I'm probably hog tied somewhere in that house!"

"Craig!" Sarah calls.

Piss off, Frank N. Furter.

"Yeah?"

"Are you back now?"

Unfortunately.

"Yeah."

"Great! Could you have a look at my bedroom for me?"

And be trapped alone with you? I'd rather nail my balls to the ceiling.

"I better finish the kitchen before starting on anywhere else in the house. One job at a time."

"Oh, yes. Of course. Is your... friend going to be alright going home?"

"Fine. A friend of ours only works around the corner, they're dropping her home. I better get those units finished.

* * *

I check my phone after Tiffy drives me home.

Craig

I want kinky sex for a month to make up for this!

You

Work cannot be that bad xxx

Craig

You gave me a raging boner and sent me into the rocky horror picture show! Not cool, babe!

You

Define kinky xxx

Craig

After today I'm thinking bondage, nipple clamps, gimp suits, the whole nine yards!

You

I was thinking... whipped cream, handcuffs, blindfolds etc xxx

Craig

You're killing me, babe!

You

I picked you up a little something on my way home today XXX

Craig

Do tell xxx

I snap a quick picture and send it over to him, awaiting the reply that comes through almost instantly.

Craig

Are they crotchless panties? xxx

You

Yep, you like? XXX

No reply. Hmm, he must have got caught up finishing the kitchen.

Screw it!

I strip down, with no plans of going back out today, I refuse to wear a bra when I don't need to. My phone pings.

Craig

On the way xxx

LOTTIE

"Strong heartbeat, always a good sign," the doctor tells us as she moves the apparatus around my belly. The liquid is cold and jellified. I'm a bag of nerves today, I just want everything to be alright. "Are we finding out what we're having today?"

Craig gives me an expectant look. He said he's fine with not finding out. Now that the opportunity is presenting itself, I can see he's changing his mind.

"No, we want it to be a surprise."

"Ooh, very nice. I think it's lovely to have that surprise on the day!" she grins, then turns to the screen. " I just need you to turn away from the screen for a second, so we don't spoil the surprise."

"No peeking!"

"I wasn't," Craig insists.

"Liar."

"I was... stretching."

"At least if you're going to lie to me, do it well."

The doctor's shoulders shake with silent laughter, she is used to us by now, or at least, she should be.

"Everything looks great, Charlotte, you and the baby are right on track. They're measuring fine and everything looks good, keep doing what you're doing, it won't be long until your little bundle is here."

"That's good to hear."

"The girls at the desk will sort you out with your next appointments. I'll see you both soon. Nearly there."

"That's great, thank you," Craig beams.

"So, what now?" I ask him, cleaning off the gel from my belly and fixing my top in place. Glancing at the clock I notice it is only quarter-to-ten.

"Are you going back to Poppintree?"

"A snowball's chance in hell of that happening today. You teased the ever-loving hell out of me yesterday, I've to make sure you pay for that."

"I thought you did that last night?"

"Not enough."

"Actually... I think I'll be the one making you pay today."

Craig cocks an eyebrow, intrigued.

"You are constantly flirted with it in front of me. I can't be having that."

"What do you have in mind?"

"You'll find out when I get you home."

A low growl escapes him. He stays silent while I make my next appointment.

* * *

Our mouths meet in a crush of want and heat. I pull my shirt overhead, feeling Lottie's hand run over my chest, down to the button on my jeans.

"I'm going to need those pants off now," she declares.

Pushing down my pants and boxers, I step out of them, stiff and throbbing. Lottie pushes me back on the bed, launching herself on my lap she kisses me greedily.

"I've got something for you."

"I can't wait," pulling her lips back to mine, she moans then pulls away, reaching for the nightstand.

"Handcuffs... you were serious about that?" I ask, looking at the bracelets dangling from her index finger.

"Yeah, it will be fun."

She's not wrong there, though the thoughts of not being able to touch her will drive me insane.

Grinning, I present my wrists to her, Lottie puts the cuffs around to spindle by the headboard securing my hands above my head.

She mounts me, sinking down, taking the full length of my cock. I attempted to move my arms to touch her, the handcuffs rattle overhead, taunting me. I can't fucking do it. Bollocks. I hate this already.

She starts to ride me in long strokes. I want to reach out, grab her by those hips and pull her down on top of me while she moves.

Lottie rolls her hips, my head tilts back on a moan. The handcuffs are the first thing I see. This is not going to work.

"You look so sexy like that," admiring the Goddess on top of me, I bite my lower lip.

She increases her pace.

"Yeah, that's it. Ride me, baby," I try to reach out and touch her. I can't. I hate this. It's infuriating. The noise of the cuffs rattling against the bed, and seeing Lottie in full control of me is turning me feral.

Leaning forward, attempting to kiss her, Lottie pulls back, smiling victoriously.

"Lottie, stop fucking teasing me!" I try to move forward, feeling the chains of the cuffs pull against the spiral on the bed. She moves back again, delighting in tormenting me. "That's it!"

Two hard tugs and the link snaps. I'm free! Lottie squeals, pausing in shock.

"I didn't say stop," I smack her hard on the ass, she yelps.

* * *

My knees press into the mattress on either side of him. Craig takes hold of my hips, his grip firm and commanding as he thrusts into me. His eyes have darkened with near mindless desire. He's going to break the bed again, isn't he?

Craig latches onto my neck, sucking hard. His hand slips up my back and grips my shoulders, pulling me down for a kiss. He rocks his hips up at the same time, sliding deep inside.

I pushed him down on the bed, bracing my hands on his shoulders, increasing the pace. His fingers bite into my thighs as I move, his grip is hard enough to leave marks.

Sensations slam through me with every roll of my hips. I slow down, attempting to curb them.

Wrapping my hair around his fist, Craig smiles as he tugs, drawing out a moan. I start up a rhythm, steadying myself on his chest. As I lift up and down, Craig throws his head back, his face twists into an expression of intense pleasure.

Soon, he bolts upright, grabbing my waist, he begins furiously rocking his hips into me. His body gleams with sweat. Tilting his hips, his demanding thrusts are angled, rubbing against somewhere unspeakably satisfying, my nails rake across his back and chest as I feel a familiar heat buildup.

The bed scrapes along the floor, I can see us moving further from the wall and right into oblivion.

The orgasm slams into me, my nails bite into his flesh, Craig roars out soon after. He collapses back on the bed, his muscles relaxing in sheer relief. Feeling myself go limp, I fall against his chest panting.

We find the key for the cuffs and take them from Craig's wrists. He holds me in against him while we lay there in content silence.

Opening my eyes I realise that I fell asleep. His phone's

vibrating on the nightstand, of course, he's sleeping through it. I glance at him, admiring the play of light and his body before answering his phone.

"Hello?"

"Oh? Hi, sorry... I think I dialled the wrong number."

"You're looking for Craig Barnes?"

"Yeah," the very feminine voice verifies.

"You have the right number. I'll get him now. Can I ask who's calling?"

"Linda Hawthorn."

Linda? As in Michael's Linda?

"Hold on a sec..." I put the phone on hold and nudge Craig.

"Five more minutes," he rolls on his side, pulling the pillow over his head. The covers slip away, exposing that biteable ass.

"It's Linda Hawthorn."

"Huh?" He peeks up over the pillow, eyes barely open. I wave the phone, waiting for the words to register. "Oh!" Pushing himself up in the bed, he takes the phone. "Hello?"

"It's still on hold, genius."

"Ah, shit... hello? Hi Linda. No, it's not a bad time. Uh-huh. How did that happen?" Pushing himself from the bed, he staggers out of the room. "The floors come with a ten-year guarantee. I can ring and get a replacement for that. No, it's no trouble at all. You may want to think of tiles in its place if you're thinking of keeping that dishwasher there though, just in case something like this happens again. OK. Yeah sure. Eh... today?"

I pull on a robe and pass him on the landing. The light from the windows highlights his face, his abs, his perfect bare body.

The kitchen is calling my name. I'm starving.

"Let me see what I can do and I'll let you know. OK, bye."

"Is everything alright?" I call upstairs, hearing Craig sigh and his footsteps stomp around.

"Her dishwasher broke down, flooded a good chunk of the kitchen. The new floors I put down are destroyed."

"Oh no, that big of a leak?"

"I know, a nightmare," he comes downstairs in his work gear, still rubbing his eyes.

"It couldn't wait until tomorrow?"

"I'm back at Frank N. Furter's tomorrow, your mom's on Wednesday, and Josie has made driving miss Daisy around all day Thursday."

"What about Friday?"

"I was hoping to get more work done in our house," he yawns, making his way into the kitchen.

"Oh right, I see..."

"You ok?"

"Fine."

"Liar," he purrs.

"I just thought we could spend the day together. You're constantly working lately."

"I know, I'm sorry. I'll make it up to you I swear. It's a two-second job today. I won't even be long, just going to assess the damage and make a call."

"It's fine. I know work comes first."

"Lottie," using the tips of his fingers, he tilts my head back. "You come first. You and our baby," he leans in, kissing me sweetly. "Come with me."

"What?"

"Come with me, it's a quick job like I said. I won't be long, then we can go out for lunch or something, yeah?"

"Doesn't it look a bit dodgy bringing your girlfriend to a job with you?"

"I'm doing her a favour on my day off, nothing dodgy about it."

"Alright, just give me a second to get dressed."

"Take your time."

I seriously hate this. It's not like I'm not used to women throwing themselves Craig, I've witnessed it for years.

I wait in the van, and as soon as she opens the door, she throws her arms around him like he's her Knight in shining armour. Hugging him a bit too tightly for my liking.

Craig says something to her and she looks my way. I offer her a weak smile in response and she hurries him inside.

Stepping out of the van to stretch my legs and catch sight of them through the large bay window. She's hanging back, letting him walk ahead, no doubt sizing him up.

"Char?"

I grow cold, I know that voice anywhere. It raises the bumps on my arms. "Michael!"

"What are you doing here?"

"Craig got a call— wait— what are you doing here? I thought you said you knew she was cheating on you?"

"I do."

"And you stay?"

"I have no proof. As I said to you before, it's not like I don't deserve it after what I did to you," I feel his eyes scan me from head to toe. "Why are you waiting out here?"

"Craig said it would be a quick job..."

"So he left you in the van? Come on," he nods to the front door, I think that's my cue to follow him.

"What?"

"Come on in, you can wait inside."

"That's not necessary."

"You're pregnant, and from the look of things, your

ankles are swelling. The least you can do is get comfortable while you wait."

I can't argue with that.

I follow Michael inside. Linda is standing a little too close to Craig when we enter the kitchen. Michael places a chaste kiss on her cheek. Craig's back is towards us. I don't think he has registered us yet.

"Would you like a drink?" Michael asks.

Craig's head snaps around to see Michael and me standing behind him, his nostrils flaring.

"I'm good, thanks."

"You're here early," Linda says.

"Got everything done by lunchtime, thought I would surprise you. That's not a problem is it?" Michael asks.

"Not at all."

"Have you met Charlotte, Craig's girlfriend," Michael gestures to me.

"I don't believe we have been formally introduced, I'm Linda," she pulls her eyes away from my boyfriend's ass long enough to register that I exist.

"Hi...Lottie... we spoke on the phone."

"I can have those floors in by next week at the latest and start then if that works?" Craig remains professional.

"That would be great, I can't believe it got so wet."

Wait, is she serious right now or is this just a horrible attempt at flirting?

"That tends to happen when something floods," Michael says flatly.

"You know what I mean. I wasn't expecting a gush like that," she gestures wildly with her arms at her ruined floors.

"Were you expecting the machine to leak? It's brand new, much like your floors, seems bit..." Michael shrugs, "weird."

"I know, just my luck. Good thing they were both

under warranty."

"And good thing that Craig is so eager to help a client in need I suppose."

"Craig is good at what he does, Michael. He always goes the extra mile for his clients," I say defensively.

"He is very thorough," Linda agrees.

Excuse you? What does she mean by that? I glance at Michael who offers me a knowing look in response. "Nice choice of words," he snorts. "Are you sure I can get you anything, Char?"

"She's fine," Craig steps up beside me.

"Coming from the man who left his pregnant girlfriend alone outside without so much as a drink."

"Michael!" Linda snaps.

"Didn't even offer the poor girl some tea or chance to sit in while she waits," Michael continues. Linda's guilty eyes find Craig who looks like he's going to smash Michael through the floor.

"No need. I know what needs doing. we can go now... Lottie," Craig nods to the door. "Linda, I'll let you know when those replacements come in and arrange to start then.

"Perfect, thank you."

* * *

I don't know what that little weasel is playing at but he is starting to get on my nerves. Lottie is uncharacteristically quiet when we get back to the van.

"Are you OK?"

"Fine." She doesn't even look at me.

"Lottie?"

"I'm fine."

Yeah? Because you really sound it! Deep breaths, it's

just the hormones. "Where do you want to go for food?"

"I'm not that hungry now."

Since when? "Are you mad at me for something?"

"No. Why would I be mad at you?"

"That's why I'm asking."

"I'm just not hungry, OK!"

"Yeah, OK... home then?"

She nods, not even bothering to look at me. What the hell have I done to piss her off?

"I love you."

"Yeah, you too."

That settles it then, she's pissed.

I've got the silent treatment all afternoon, I've tried to talk to her but other than a few grunts or one-line retorts Lottie hasn't spoken to me. My phone pings and I welcome the distraction, still not sure what it is that I've done to make her so mad at me.

> Unknown
>
> Does your relationship come with a warranty? ;)

Michael. That son of a bitch.

CRAIG

"Sabotage," Jay grunts.

"Definitely," Dylan agrees, "he's a slimy bastard."

"Lottie is vulnerable right now with the hormones and all. Despite everything, they do have history," Jay cautions.

"Meaning?"

"Meaning even if she doesn't want to hear him out, whatever he's saying to her is going to play on her mind. You need to make sure you can squish whatever doubts he is tossing at her," Dylan advises.

"I would if I knew what it was he was saying. She won't tell me!"

"He did the dirt on her when he was away working, right? I mean before he got caught," Jay queries.

"Yeah."

"Well, there you go."

"I'm not cheating on Lottie!"

"We never said you were, but it makes sense doesn't it? We work long hours. You've seen how desperate some of these women are, practically sit in our laps when they offer to make us a cuppa. It's not a hard push to say it could happen if you wanted it to."

"Isn't that how you got with Olivia?" Dylan asks, taking a drag from his smoke and blowing the fumes out the window.

"I— shut up! That was years ago and it lasted a wet weekend."

"Yeah, but it did happen because an attractive woman offered herself up on her plate to you while you were working."

"I never cheated on anyone though, we were both single!"

The insinuation is really pissing me off. I've never cheated.

"Doesn't matter, there's a possibility there and in Lottie's head, Michael already screwed her over when he was "working long hours" and you have been with women that were clients of ours when we first started. You need to do some serious damage control," Jay sighs, checks his mirrors, and indicates to the inside lane.

"Not to mention pregnancy hormones make women crazy as it is," Dylan snorts.

"But I wouldn't—"

"We know. Look I'll have Tiffy have a word with Lottie on the weekend, yeah? You know women. She will sooner listen to her friends and anything with a dick."

"We are the enemy right now. A word of advice don't go to Linda's house alone," Dylan adds.

"What?"

"Think about it, Michael has access to the house, he's trying to stitch you up as the bad guy here. Linda seems like a lovely girl but two marbles rolling about in a tin can, if she spent more time with her head in a book than in getting her lips done, she might have something going on there."

"She's a natural flirt, she has done it to all of us but we aren't the ones who are going to look like assholes if we're working on the house alone," Jay explains.

"Yeah, if he is setting you up like this, imagine how easy it would be to get a suspicious-looking picture with you two looking cozy. All it takes is a right angle and an offer of a cuppa and you're fucked if you have no one to back you up."

I sit in the passenger seat of Jay's car. Chewing my bottom lip and staring into the horizon. "But... if Lottie doesn't trust me... there's no point in us being together." My heart sinks at the thought. I love Lottie with everything in me. I always have. I always will. She's the mother of my child, if she doesn't trust me, the relationship is doomed, right? What's the point in defending myself and taking precautions just to be seen as guilty no matter what I do.

* * *

"Trust him to forget his wallet!" Tiffy growls.

"You act like he did it on purpose."

"Didn't he? Any excuse to look at my ass."

"Take the next left here," I point to the upcoming turn.

"Why buy your house down the arse end of nowhere?"

"Clearly not a people person."

"Soooo, Craig then..." Tiffy snorts.

"Probably."

"Everything OK with you two?"

"I guess."

"What happened? He go in the wrong hole or something?" Tiffy shifts gears, slowing down as we get closer to our destination.

"Tiffy!"

"Lottie, come on. Talk to me."

"I just— how do you do it?"

"Do Craig? I don't know. I imagine I'd have to lure him in dressed as Wonder Woman or something."

"I'm serious!"

"Clearly."

"How do you do it with Jay?" *Your destination is on the right,* the sat NAV announces. Tiffany slows the car to a stop, as soon as we pull up there is a woman practically dangling off Jason's arm. Her outfit might as well be painted on.

"Who's this bitch?" Tiffy zones in immediately.

"Exactly my point! How do you do it?"

"Watch and learn," Tiffany gets out of the car, not at all glamorous like the woman vying for Jason's attention. Tiffy's chocolate brown hair has been swept in a ponytail, she's wearing leggings and an oversized top but she walks like she belongs on a runway. Jay turns and sees Tiffy coming towards him, seemingly relieved.

Tiffy reaches out, grabbing him by his shirt, pulling him in for a fierce kiss. "Where would you be without me?" she snakes her arms around his waist, tugging him closer and shooting the other woman a dangerous smile.

"Lost that's for sure," Jay smirks, "you're a saint, babe."

"And you will remember that by getting on your knees tonight." The woman scoffs and stomps off to look for a new victim. "And that, Lottie, is how we handle the slappers."

"Is Craig around?" I ask.

"If he has any sense, I'd say he found a good hiding spot inside that house," Jay chuckles.

"Do you mind if I—

"Go on in, Lottie, just watch your step, debris every-where," Dylan announces.

"Thank you."

I slowly ascend the staircase, Dylan wasn't kidding the place looks like a storm blew through here. I hear him before I see him.

"I know, I know. Of course, I love her."

He's talking about me?

"What's the point? I'm better off ending it..."

I feel my heart twist in my chest, my breath catching in my throat. I want the ground to open and swallow me whole. Craig's ending things? He's breaking up with me? Tears prick my eyes. I can't do this, not here. I hurry back down the stairs, needing air. Needing to escape.

"Lottie?" Tiffy asks.

"I need to go."

"What happened?"

"Just... please, can we go?"

"Yeah, sure."

"Lottie?" Jays asks, his brow furrowing with concern.

* * *

"Josie, I'll call you back."

Lottie? I could have sworn I just heard Jay calling her. I walk to the window and see her jumping into the car with Tiffy, she looks flustered.

Taking the stairs two at a time I bound out of the house just as Tiffy drives off.

"What happened? Why was Lottie here?"

"She came with Tiffy to drop off my wallet," Jay explains.

"She went inside looking for you and next thing I know she's running for the car," Dylan says.

She went inside? Shit! Did she hear me on the phone? I dial her number and she rejects it on the second ring. Shit! I try again, rejected again. "Come on, Lottie," she switched her phone off. "I gotta go."

"Is everything, OK?" Jay presses.

"No! I gotta go! Shit, you drove today! Tiffy! Get her to come back!"

Jay dials Tiffy's number without asking any questions. "Hey, babe... can you come back? Breaking up with her—"

"No! It's not like that, it's a mistake!"

"Did you get that? Yeah, well can't she at least talk to him? I mean, I get that she's upset but I think— why are you biting the arse off me for? I didn't say it!" Jay pulls the phone away and stuffs it back in his pocket. "She hung up."

"You're breaking up with Lottie?" Dylan gasps.

"No! I mean, I was talking to Josie, she overheard... I was just ranting, I didn't mean I was going to do it!"
I try Lottie again, her phone is still off so I try another number.

"Hello?"

"Nick! Nick, I just fucked up!"

"Who did you kill?" he snorts.

"No! With Lottie, I fucked up!"

"What did you do?" his tone turns more serious.

"Not what you're thinking so drop the fucking attitude! It's Michael..."

"Again!"

"I know, spare me the lecture."

"I told you what he's like!"

"I know, I know, shut up and listen," I explain the situation to him, and in all fairness, he listens to everything I have to say.

"Yeah, you fucked up."

"I didn't know she was coming near the house! That was not a conversation I wanted her to hear, if it was I would have said it to her by now," I'm burning a hole in the concrete right now with my pacing.

"I've done the same with Abbie when she's pissing me off. I'll have a word with Lottie."

"Thank you!"

Jay drives me home, the one time I decide to fucking carpool and this happens!

"Lottie," no sign of her downstairs. "Baby?" I barely remember running up the stairs, the next thing I know I'm in our room. Something is off, I can't put my finger on it right away.

There's a note on the bed. Unfolding the paper her appointment card for the next checkup falls out and the baby sonogram. The note itself is blank.

I turn for the stairs, noticing about halfway down that her house keys are on the floor as if she's put it back through the letterbox. Shit!

With my heart in my throat, I turn back upstairs to our room. Now I know what's off. Lottie's things, they're gone.

She thought I was leaving her, and instead, she's just gone and left me.

LOTTIE

*T*ears free flow down my face, hitting the pillow.

"Do you not think you acted a bit... rash?"

"Oh sure, take his side!"

"Lottie, have you at least talked to him?"

"And say what, mom? He wanted to leave me, so I made it easy on him. He doesn't have to worry about me moving out—"

"That baby..." mom reasons.

"I won't stop him from being there for the baby but he doesn't need to feel stuck with me now."

"Lottie—"

"No, mom!"

"He loves you."

"Yeah? Because it really fucking sounded like it!"

"Are you sure you heard him right?"

"So now I'm pregnant and hard of hearing, thanks for that!"

"No, I mean—"

"I want to be alone."

"Lottie..."

"Please."

Mom sighs, "OK, love. I'll be downstairs if you need me." After the door clicks shut, I turn my phone on. Twelve missed calls from Craig, three from Nick, six texts. Where to start?

"About damn time!" Nick barks.

"I'm not in the mood."

"Where are you?"

"Moms."

"Look, about Craig—"

"I don't want to talk about it."

"Lottie, just listen—"

"No! You didn't want us together from the start, you got your wish."

Nick says nothing for a moment. "You're right, I didn't want you together," he admits. "Craig is one of my best friends, and you're my little sister. It's weird, and today is a perfect example of why I didn't want you to happen. I didn't want to be put in this position."

"Well, I'm sorry for being an inconvenience to you!"

"Lottie, talk to him."

"No," I don't care if I sound like a stroppy teenager right now, Craig broke my heart today.

"Woman up, and talk to him."

"Why do I have to do it?"

"Because he's been trying to call you and you won't answer, so now, it's on you."

"He wanted to be rid of me," I'm snarling at the phone, I don't know why. It's not like we are face-timing. He can't see me, my venom is wasted.

"Bullshit!"

"I heard him—"

"The same way I heard Abbie saying she will smother me with a pillow if I kept her awake snoring. The same way Abbie told me that mom hates me and pays her money to look after me because she wouldn't want me back? The same way Tiffy told you she was going to bury Jason out the back garden if he didn't take her on a weekend away?"

"What you getting at?"

"You're in a relationship, a proper non-toxic relationship, for once. Guess what, you're going to piss each other off. You're going to rant and vent to friends and family when something is going on, that doesn't mean you will follow through with it. It's said in anger and irritation!"

"Mom wouldn't take you back. You're a pig, she wouldn't clean up after you again."

"Glad to see that you're listening to me," Nick chuckles. "Do you trust Craig?"

"What?"

"You heard, do you trust him?"

"Of course I do but—"

"No buts, you either trust him, or you don't," he sounds so much like dad right now.

"Women throw themselves at him all the time..."

"They have been doing that since I've known him, probably even longer," Nick reasons.

"He could be tempted..."

"The same way I could have taken that prostitute up on a ride in the back of the car the other day, that doesn't mean I did it."

"I fucking hope not," I snort and lean back against the wall.

"Lottie—"

"I mean, she'd be riddled."

"Getting a little off-topic here."

"Working gals wouldn't have crabs, they'd have lobsters."

"And, she's off."

"Don't be shellfish."

"For fuck's sake," I can hear him grinning.

"I'm scared, Nick," wiping my tears away with my sleeve, I shift on the bed, trying to get comfortable.

"Nothing to be scared of."

"Birth."

"Bar that."

"I'm not good enough for him."

"Says who?"

"I see the looks we get when we're together, people wondering what he's doing with me. I'm hardly glamorous."

"Lottie, you're beautiful. You're funny... wildly inappropriate and have a mouth that could make a sailor blush. I've seen the girls Craig has dated, I've seen him with them he's never looked at one of them the same way he looks at you."

"You're just saying that because you're my brother."

"No, it's my job to stick you in a headlock and give you a swirly, compliments are not part of the job description. Talk to him."

"And say what?"

"Try to refrain from using the term ass. I'd say that's a good start."

"That will never work."

"Not with you it won't."

I try to steady my breathing, "I left."

"I know."

"How is he?"

"Distraught, confused, angry. All the above."

I gulp back a lump in my throat. "I didn't want to hurt him."

"I know, only you can fix this now."

"K, I'll try." Taking a deep breath in I dial Craig's number with trembling hands.

Voicemail, fan-fucking-tastic.

"Hi... it's me. I... emm... I spoke to Nick, and... can... can we maybe talk? K, bye."Well, that was awkward as hell and that was just a voicemail.

I rest my head against the wall and close my eyes. I'm an idiot. I should have got Tiffy to turn the car back to hear Craig out. I should have stayed and confronted him rather than running like a coward.

My phone buzzes and my heart skips a beat. "Hey..."

"Hi," his voice is gruff.

"Craig. I'm sorry... I—"

"You left."

"I thought—"

"I followed you home. Left the job. But I was too late. You were gone," there is something new in his voice, a sort of pain I've never heard from him before.

"I was upset. I—"

"Didn't even give me the chance to explain," he sounds

miserable.

My throat feels like I've swallowed a razor blade. "I'm sorry."

"Me too. I thought we had something..."

"Craig, I love you."

He sucks in a breath, his voice cracking. "I love you, too. But you left me, Lottie."

"I thought you were leaving me!"

"The same way you think that I would cheat on you?" there it is, that hurt in his voice, it's agonising to hear.

"I-I panicked."

"Why didn't you talk to me?"

"I was afraid," I admit, feeling tears prick my eyes again.

"Do you honestly think I would do that to you? Hurt you like that?"

"No!"

"I want to believe you."

"But you don't."

"How can I?"

"I messed up. I let my insecurities get the better of me. I'm sorry. I don't want this to end..."

"You have a funny way of showing it," his pain turns to venom, I can't blame him for being mad at me.

"I'm sorry," tears fall from my eyes once again. I've really made a mess of things.

"I don't want this to end either," he admits. "But we will never work if you don't trust me."

"I do! I do trust you, Craig! I swear I do. I panicked. I was afraid of history repeating itself, and I ran. I'm a coward. I know," it's only then that I realise my biggest mistake. Craig's dad left when times got hard. I ran and left without warning. I walked out on Craig. I didn't realise I did the very thing his father did to him. I left without explanation. I fucked this up. I've cut him deeply with this. I hate myself for doing it.

"Craig, please... I made a mistake, I wasn't thinking. I'm

so sorry, please. You're the best thing to happen to me. You're my best friend." ·

"I don't know if I can, Lottie."

"I understand," dare God the pain. Every one of my heartstrings is breaking right now. I've no one to blame but myself. Craig. The love of my life. I've lost him. I can barely breathe, the pain is excruciating. "I'll get Nick to bring me by and collect the rest of my things by the end of the week." I don't wait for a reply I hang up and sob into my hands. I've messed up. I've lost my best friend and boyfriend with one stupid decision.

* * *

The sheets still smell like her. I've lived in this house for six years and right now, it feels alien.

No sounds.

No mess.

No Lottie.

The sapphire in Josie's ring sparkles in the sunlight, I twirl it around in my fingers. I was going to propose.

She said she's sorry, I believe she is. But what's to stop her from doing it again? Running as soon as we hit another rough patch. Lottie is the only girl I ever truly loved. Coming home to find she just left, she didn't even try, didn't give me a chance to explain... didn't even fight for us. But she admitted she messed up. I guess I did too, in a way.

I thought I was protecting her by keeping those phone calls secret, lying about them. I can see why she thought something was going on. I've never been able to lie to her.

She was afraid, and she ran. I'm afraid, and now I'm keeping her at arm's length. How am I any better?

I pick up the picture of peanut and stare at it. They deserve their parents, both of us, not a broken home. Lottie and I— we have a lot of shit that we need to work through, then again, who doesn't?

I can't deny this baby a chance of having mom and dad under the same roof, the same way I can't just walk away, not from Lottie. I want to make it work. I'm desperately in love with her. The stunt she pulled, although leaving me livid, has done nothing to stop my feelings for her.

I pick up the phone and I'm instantly greeted by a picture of me and Lottie in bed. She's curled up against me with her just fucked hair fanned over the pillow, smiling up at me. We look happy. We were happy.

You

You're at your moms?

Lottie

Yeah

You

On the way

CRAIG

After a long frank and emotional conversation, Lottie agreed to come home. I've had breakups that were less devastating than that discussion, but here we are, back home and things are a little off, to say the least.

It's like she's afraid to ask me to do anything for her. Usually, I make several trips downstairs for her because she doesn't want to get up and get her own snacks. Since she's come home, Lottie hasn't asked me for a thing.

I shower alone, undisturbed. Another strange occurrence. If she's not in the shower with me, Lottie is normally perched on the counter, or standing against the door waffling the ears off me. When I come out, I notice the light on in her old room.

Pushing the door open, I find her on the bed reading. "Are you OK?"

"Yeah, why?" her head pokes out from behind the book.

"What are you doing in here?" She holds up the book as if I'm stupid for even asking her. "Is there something wrong with our bed?"

"Oh, I thought—"

"You thought what?"

She blushes to her roots, gets up, and walks into our room without saying anything more.

"Lottie?"

"Are you hungry?" her voice comes out a pitch too high.

"Huh?"

"I can order out if you are."

"I'm fine, thanks."

"Oh, OK."

I dry off and get into bed noticing Lottie is right on the edge. "Nausea?"

"No."

"Afraid I'll bite?"

"What? No!" she giggles nervously.

"Well, I just had a shower, so I know I don't smell."

"What are you on about?"

"Why are you all the way over there?"

She turns her head, frowning, seemingly only noticing how close to the edge she actually is. "Oh!"

"What's going on with you?"

"I don't know," she starts crying.

I freeze, what the hell brought that on? "Me?" I ask.

"No."

"Heartburn?"

"No."

"Nipples? I'm running out of options here, Lottie, give me something."

"Why do you love me?"

"What?"

"Why me? You can have anyone you want. Why settle for me?" she's in hysterics now. I'm still looking at her like the elephant man's staring back at me. What the hell did she just say? Did she just ask me that?

Her skin is red and blotchy, her hair frizzy and she has snot-free-flowing from her nose just as quickly as the tears stream from her eyes. "Settle?" I echo.

"Yes! You settled for me..."

"Since when?"

"Craig, I'm being serious!"

"So am I! How have I settled? In what warped world are you living in? Settled for you? Are you fucking serious?"

"You could do better."

"Says who?"

"Everyone! I see the looks we get when we're together, people wondering what the hell you see in me..."

"This has to be the baby brain talking, right? You're not actually this psychotic?"

"Craig!"

"Lottie, you're fucking beautiful! Stunning! How are you so deluded that you don't see that? Nobody I have met compares to you, there's no other woman out there that can hold a fucking candle to you. You're beautiful, kind, funny, smart, sexy as hell, the best sex I've had—women like you don't exist, believe me, I've spent years looking! You think I settled for you? Baby, I hit the jackpot... well," I scan her over, "for most of it, right now you look like you belong in the Blair Witch."

She laughs, wiping her face with the sleeve of her oodie.

"As far as I'm concerned, other women stopped existing the second I met you." What sort of Nazi brainwashing did Michael do on her?

Pulling her into my lap, I hold her close. Her breathing begins to steady, I feel the baby kicking at me and can't help but smile.

My beautiful hot mess of a girlfriend, she's strong in so many ways, it's easy to forget that she was neglected in the past, abused emotionally, mentally. I've half a mind to staple Michael's balls to his legs for all he did to her. I'm tempted to hit the prick with the van for all to shit he has caused, trying to come between us.

I won't let that happen she's my woman, that's my baby, this is my family, nobody is going to target them and get away with it. That prick will soon find out that he's not the only one who can play dirty.

I fall back onto the pillows, bringing Lottie with me, one

hand on the bump, the other wraps around her waist. She falls asleep pretty quickly. I drag the blankets over her then pick up my phone.

You

Wanna play a little game?

Jay

What you thinking Jigsaw?

MICHAEL

"Ready?" Linda calls.

"You're wearing that?"

"Why? Is there something wrong?"

"It's a bit, eh... tight, don't you think?"

"Tight?"

"Never mind, I'm sure you'll be fine." I wander into the kitchen, scanning the area while Linda puts on her shoes.

"All set?"

"You want to get a coat, so you don't get a chill," she's lucky she's pretty because she's as thick as two planks.

"Good thinking!"

I listen to the clip-clop of her shoes on the floor, then reach around the washing machine and slice at the drain.

Pulling out my phone, I check Facebook, no change on Charlotte's or Craig's account. For fuck's sake, why hasn't she left him yet? Instagram. Nothing on Char's page. I click on Craig's.

The rat bastard.

His latest post is a picture of Char asleep on his chest with the caption.

Let's watch a movie she said, it will be fun she said! #pregnancy #strugglecuddle #I'mjustthatcomfortable.

Pulling out my other phone, I power it on. Her image stares back at me. Charlotte's. A bright smile meets her dazzling sea-green eyes. I took this picture about four years ago on a night out, just before *he* happened. I saw the way he looked at her. Saw the way she looked at him. I knew something was going on, but she kept denying it, said they were just friends. Yeah... *friends.* As soon as we split he took her in with open arms.

Screw it!

> **You**
>
> You cannot have her!

> **Asshat**
>
> Too late :D

> **You**
>
> Leave!

> **Asshat**
>
> Make me.

> **You**
>
> I don't want to have to hurt you!

> **Asshat**
>
> I wish I could say the same

"All set this time, I swear!"

I power off my phone and shove it in my coat. "Great, let's go."

The door barely opens when I hear Linda gasp. "Oh my goodness..."

"WHAT THE HELL!" My car has been vandalised. The tires sliced, the wing mirrors ripped off and a sick smiley face sprayed in red all over the bonnet.

Barnes! I know this was him!

Pulling out my phone, I log onto Instagram.

Another picture has gone up of Craig and Lottie snuggled up together, with the caption:

Pizza is on its way, she will wake then! Nothing better than a night in with the other half #comfort #provemewrong

The bastard!

"Will I call the police?" Linda asks. "Michael?"

"Go on inside, I'll make the call," pulling out my spare phone from my coat pocket, I power it on and log on to last calls.

"Hello, sunshine!" his voice booms over the phone.

"You rat bastard!"

"Kiss your mother with that mouth?"

"You'll pay for this, I know it was you."

"Know what was me?" I can hear the smug grin on his face over the phone.

"I'm calling the police!"

"Go ahead."

"Don't think I won't!"

"I'm quaking in the jocks right now."

"You stupid son-of-a-bitch! You came here and vandalised my—"

"I haven't left the house all evening."

"I know it was you!"

"Prove me wrong, Michael. Prove. Me. Wrong," the phone hangs up.

I don't believe this! I reported the vandalism to the police and who should show up, only Nick!

"Well, there is nothing more we can do bar file a report..." he stands like a typical cop, shoulders back, erect spine, strong stance.

"It was Barnes!"

"Did you see him do it?"

"No."

"Did anyone see him do it?"

"No."

"Was he here earlier? Did you see him around here at all today?"

"No. I know it was him!"

Nick pulls out his phone, logging on to Instagram. "It couldn't have been him, look," he points the phone at me. "He's been at home all evening from the look at things."

This is a setup, that bastard wants Char to himself, I need him away from her! I need to put a wedge in before that baby is born. Charlotte will never leave without the baby, never. He'll have leverage. My leverage. She is mine. That baby belongs to me, part of it anyway. The Charlotte part. Does that prick think he can destroy all the work I've put in over the years? Take my property and start over, no. I won't allow it.

"That's wrong! It's wrong! I know he did it!"

"It looks like Craig has a solid alibi for this, Michael. Sorry, there is nothing else I can do bar file a report," he jots something down then his eyes flick up to me. "Why would Craig have it out for you anyway?"

"He hates me."

"He doesn't even know you, not really."

"He's jealous."

"Of you?" the bastard has a condescending smile on his face.

"I've been talking to Charlotte, he doesn't like it. Obviously threatened of me."

"Is that so? They never mentioned anything."

"He's no good for her, Nick. He's toxic!"

"Funny, I remember saying the same about you. Now, if you excuse me, duty calls.

* * *

I slept like a baby last night. Best night sleep I've had in a long time.

I got a call from Linda this morning, something about

her washing machine leaking and destroying more of her floors. There's a surprise. She claims to have bad luck. I liked it think of him as a plague.

"There are certain songs you have to finish," Lottie insists.

"Whatever you say, baby."

"Don't believe me? Fine!" She inhales dramatically, "Country Rooooads, take me hooooome...."

"I'm not doing it!" I protest, clamping the wheel.

"To a plaaaace, I belooong..."

" *West Virginia!* Bollocks!"

"Heeeeey, hey baby!"

"Ooh ah!"

"Ooh eee ooh ah ah..."

"Ting Tang Walla Walla Bing bang!"

"I rest my case."

"I feel violated..." I snort.

"You wish!"

"I kinda do, yeah," the phone buzzes, "can you get that, babe?"

"Sure! Hello?"

"Luscious Lottie!"

"Down boy!" I scoff.

"Hi, Jay!"

"Fathead can hear me, yeah?"

"Loud and clear," I smirk, checking the mirrors and indicating to turn off the motorway.

"That's taken care of."

"Grand, thanks."

"Anytime!"

"What's taking care of?" Lottie presses.

Jay just about keeps the sniggering to a minimum as he says "Erectile dysfunction, did you know that they made a pill for that?"

"I never would have guessed."

Jason snorts over the phone, "when's the next orgy?"

"Can't be tomorrow, I have my baby shower then."

"So, just me and Craig bunking up then, yeah?"

"You can have the floor!" I call.

"Now come on, I heard brokeback mountain is on Netflix. I bought matching cowboy boots!"

"I'm hanging up now."

"You wouldn't dare!"

I reach for the phone in Lottie's hand and hang up.

"That wasn't very nice."

"It's fine, it's just Jay," I pull into the car park and wait for Lottie to waddle into the shopping center. "Fill your basket, it's on me."

"What?"

"Go on."

"What do you want me to get?"

"Clothes for you, the baby, whatever. I won't say no to something particularly skimpy, your tits look amazing lately.

She looks at me as if to ask if I've gone mad. I tap her on the ass and nudge her towards the women's section. Giving her some room to browse, I find myself in amongst the baby clothes.

There are three particular baby grows that catch my attention, one that says **I try to be good but I take after my daddy.** Another, **party in my crib let's get tit-faced,** and another, **To-Do List, poop, take a nap, suck some titties.** Are they wildly inappropriate? Perhaps. Am I picking them up? You bet your sweet ass I am!

I toss in some Disney stuff so Lottie can't object and go searching for her, it's not hard to find her, she's the only one in the shop with a waddle.

* * *

That son-of-a-bitch! That rat bastard! I came into work this morning to find a box full of porn, dildos, and butt plugs sitting on my desk. Stephanie from accounting practically ran, I've been working on luring her in and that prick is after scaring her off.

Then someone sent a doctored photo of me to my boss, this screams Barnes. I know it's that prick. I just need to think of how I'm going to repay him. I need a shower to wash this day off me.

There's some post on the floor when I get in. I pick up the letters and flick through them, one letter just says my name, no address, no stamps.

"Barnes," I growl and peel open the envelope. There are pictures of me with Linda, Stephanie, Claire from the gym, and the one that makes me look twice. One of me, in a hot tub with Karen, my boss's wife. That prick has had me followed, and from the look at things, he's been doing it for weeks.

Shit!

Flipping over the picture, there is something scribbled on the back.

Final warning, asshole. Stay away.

CRAIG

"*S*o, what you're saying is, I have to clear out a room in the house?"

"The baby is soooo spoilt already, and they aren't even here yet!"

"You had a good time though, that's all that matters."

"I did, but I can't wait to get home. I miss you."

"I miss you, too. There's no one to steal the covers at night when you're not here."

"I should be back around four, give or take, mom wants us all to go for lunch and you know what that means."

"Telling stories of your little tushy from when you were a baby?"

"No, that will be Josie telling everyone about you."

"Hey, it's a good ass!"

"I never said otherwise!"

"OK, go on, enjoy. I'll cry into a cheese toasty and wait at the doorstep like a sad puppy until you come home."

"That's all I ask, love you."

"Love you, too." Hanging up the phone, I turn for the door, someone is banging the ever-loving shit out of it. Whipping the door open to see a fist travelling for my head. I dodge hearing a loud thud.

"Son-of-a-bitch!" Michael swings again, missing me by a hair's breadth. Michael makes a grab at me, attempting to seize me. He catches thin air, stumbles back into the wall spitting blood and two teeth.

"You should have stayed away!" I growl.

"Charlotte's mine!"

"Over my dead body!"

"That can be arranged," Michael dodges me as I make

a grab at him. I slam headfirst into the open door. Meeting
me when I turn, I catch Michael's fist in my throat and
crash to the earth.

A flash of light is all the warning I get, a knife slashes at
me, I catch hold of Michael's arm, the knife slicing along
my forearm in the process, the bastard has no intention of
releasing it.

Tightening my grip and with an audible crack, Michael's
arm shatters. Kicking the blade away, I wrestled him to the
floor and call Nick.

"Hello?"

"HE'S IN THE FUCKING HOUSE!" I yell at the
phone, slipping from my grasp.

"What?"

"HE'S GOT A KNIFE!" the phone hits the floor.
Michael tries to wriggle free, I slam his head into the floor,
dazing him.

"I'll be right there!"

"Char—" Michael growls.

"Shut up! Don't mention her name!"

"Get off!"

"Yeah, right. You tried to scare her away from me, tried
to split us up!"

Michael continues to fight and thrash about, trying to
wriggle free.

"When that didn't work, you come to our home with a
fucking knife!"

Throwing his head back, he catches me in the nose,
blood pours down my face. I blink back the tears, noticing
him scrambling for the blade again. Swinging my leg out it
connects with his stomach, lifting him from the floor.

"I should kill you for this!"

"You don't have the balls," Michael hisses.

"Oh, I do. Lottie could have come home, she could

have been here when you showed up." blood-drops fall from my face onto his.

"You should have stayed away from her," Michael spits.

I straddle him, my right fist shooting out, when it retracts there is blood covering my knuckles. Michael attempts to fight back but my reflexes are quicker, hitting their target every time. I dodge a fist, coming back down with my own, throwing my full body weight behind it. I hit Michael's jaw with such force, blood spatters my face.

"Craig, stop!" grabbing my arm in midair, Nick pulls me back.

My knuckles are busted open from the impact of the blows I delivered.

"He's not worth it!"

I continue to stare Michael down, he's gurgling on his own blood. I hear Nick's partner say something into the radio about an ambulance.

"I need you to come with me," Nick sighs, taking hold of my arm and leading me from the house.

* * *

"My grandbaby is on the way!" My mom shrieks excitedly. "I just cannot wait to kiss that little face!"

"Calm down, mom."

"Ah, let her gloat," Tiffy smirks.

My phone buzzes, "it's Nick," excusing myself from the table, I walk outside and take the call. "Hello?"

"Hey, it's me. Don't freak out!" Nick sounds agitated.

"What happened?"

"Craig has been arrested..."

"WHAT?" My heart starts to pound against my chest, it's suddenly painful to breathe.

"Michael came by the house. There was... an

altercation."

"Is Craig ok?"

"He's fine, playing poker in the holding cell with Graham keeping watch. Don't worry about that."

"But he's arrested?"

"Technically... yeah. It's a bollocks charge. Michael insisted on pressing charges when he came to and it's most likely going to be dropped. They have Michael on trespassing, harassment, stalking, intent to cause grievous bodily harm, the list goes on. He's screwed and he knows it."

"H-how?"

"He kept an old phone from when you were together. All those texts, phone calls, everything was on the phone. Plus the cameras Craig installed after those pictures were sent to you have him throwing the first punch, it's clearly a case of self-defense with Craig."

"And Craig is definitely OK?"

"He's not hurt, a little scuffed up but nothing compared to the state he left Michael in," Nick chuckles, it puts me at ease.

"Can I speak with him?"

"Sure, hold on a sec," I hear Nick walking, a door opening and closing, some personal greetings, and another door opening and shutting. "It's Lottie."

"Hey, baby!"

"Are you OK?"

"I'm fine!"

"You're sure?"

"Bored off my knob, but I'm good, babe, honestly."

"Will you be home soon?"

"Ehhh, will I be home soon," he directs his question to someone in the room with him. "Jury's out on that one I'm afraid. I'm hoping to get back tonight."

"What happened?"

"I don't know."

A blatant lie, but I know he can't go into details with the police there to overhear him.

"Michael just showed up, told me to stay away from you, the usual shit..."

"Then what happened?"

"I told him where to go with that and he just lost it."

And there is the truth. "You're sure you're OK?"

"Babe, I'm fine. Other than a sore ass, apparently, a cushion is too much to ask in here. I don't want you to worry. I'll be home soon, OK. I'm not sure how soon but I promise I'll be home."

"OK, love you."

"Love you, too."

"All good?" Nick asks after taking his phone back.

"Get him out of there!"

"Lottie..."

"No! I'm due this baby soon, and I'm not having a baby with a father in prison! You get him out of there Nicholas Evans or I swear to Christ I will make sure you never have sex again!"

"I don't even want to know."

"Do it!"

"Jeez, keep your knickers on!"

"TAKE THEM OFF!" Craig shouts.

"Shut up!" Nick snaps. "I'll sort it out, Lottie. I promise."

"You better."

Nick hangs up and I go back to the girls at the table.

"Is Nick OK?" mom asks.

"Yeah."

"What's up?"

"Craig's been arrested..."

"What?"

"What?" Tiffy questions.

"What!" Josie repeats.

"What!" Shannon snaps.

"Are you OK?" Katie asks.

"Fine. Michael showed up, Craig... it was self-defense..."

"And he got arrested for that?" Tiffy snaps. "Hell no!" Tiffany's on the phone to her dad in a heartbeat. "Daddy!" she takes it outside to bark orders down the phone.

"Her father is a policeman?" Josie asks.

"A judge," I confirm.

Josie lights up.

"Craig arrested..." mom sighs.

"It wouldn't be the first time. He was a bit of a hot head when he was younger after Eleanor died. He calmed down after some time, straightened up," Josie explains.

"This is my fault..."

"No, Lottie, don't even think like that," Josie puts her hand on mine and squeezes, offering me a warm smile.

"Michael is to blame, not you or Craig, Michael!" Shannon snaps.

"Shannon's right, darling," mom takes my other hand.

"If he is not out by tomorrow morning, there will be hell to pay!" Tiffy growls over the phone. Charles may be a well-respected Judge but when it comes to Tiffy, he's basically her bitch. She has him wrapped around her finger. "Daddy, please! He's my friend...Thank you, daddy," Tiffany hangs up the phone and marches back to us. "Tomorrow at the latest, or I start shooting lightning bolts out my eyes."

"Tiffy, you don't have to—"

"Quiet, fatty, and keep that baby cooking."

"Love you, too."

Mom stayed with me for most of the evening, along with Tiffy, they cleaned up the mess left behind from whatever the hell happened in the house.

I can't believe this, Michael came here intending to hurt Craig. Why would he do that? Why would he keep pictures of me? Why would he try and destroy what I have with Craig?

I feel a hard kick from the baby and rub my bump, "don't worry, little one, daddy will be home soon."

Josie doesn't seem too worried about it, as she said, she has dealt with these kinds of messes in the past. I'd love to be as cool and collected as Josie.

I hear the scrape of a key in the front door and the click of it opening. "Craig?" I hurry to the landing and look down at the person entering the house. His face is bruised and swollen, his hands inflamed with angry tears on the flesh of his knuckles.

"Craig!"

"Hey, baby!"

How the hell can he be so cheerful? He looks like he's been through the wars. "This is not a little scuffed up, what the hell happened?"

"I'm fine, honestly."

"Craig!"

"Lottie, I'm fine, baby. I promise."

"They let you go?"

"I think I have Tiffy to thank for that, and Nick, of course."

"Craig..." I reach for his face, he doesn't even wince when my fingers trace his tender flesh.

"I'm fine, baby. My ass is killing me though, plus I'm starving."

"I'll make you something to eat."

"Nah... I'll order it."

"I don't mind..."

"I do, get that gorgeous ass to bed and I'll be up in a minute."

" Josie?"

"Called her when I got out, don't worry," he smacks me on the rear and nudges me towards the stairs. I hear him place an order with the local Chinese takeaway, then he comes bounding up the stairs.

"Thirty minutes, give or take," he pulls off his shirt, his chest and sides bruised.

"Oh, my God!"

"You usually save that until my pants come off..."

"Craig!"

"Baby, I'm fine, it looks worse than it is."

"You must be so sore?"

"I would not say no to a rub down."

"Get on the bed."

"Really?" his eyes light up.

"On the bed, now."

"Yes ma'am!" Craig jumps on the bed, grinning like a Cheshire cat.

Reaching into the nightstand, I pull out a vial of lavender oil, spilling out a small amount between Craig's shoulders. I begin to massage his strained body.

With a series of smooth or rhythmic strokes, Craig begins to melt my touch. A moan escapes him as I trace slow circular patterns up and down his spine."

"Baby... that feels... so good," he lets out an appreciative moan. "Remind me to get arrested more often."

"No can't do, Batman," I continue to gradually apply pressure, rubbing out the numerous knots in his shoulders and lower back. When I can find no more, I lean in, kissing the back of his neck before climbing off.

"You've forgotten the front," he teases.

A knock comes on the door.

"Food's here!"

"Bollocks, I was enjoying that."

"Now you gotta go and answer the door with a semi."

Craig looks down and laughs, he turns to answer the door and calls me down after he takes the food in. "I assumed you'd be hungry," he says as he grabs some plates.

"Love you!"

"Was that your phone?" he asks, glancing at my phone on the end of the counter. "I thought I heard your phone going off."

"I didn't hear anything..." I turn to check. "Nope not my—"

Craig is looking at me, arms outstretched, holding a ring. Josie's ring. I know that ring!

"Craig..."

"I was going to wait to do this, but after everything that's happened I don't want to wait any longer," he drops to his knee. His grey eyes sparkling like the sapphire in his hands.

"Craig your hands... you're shaking."

"I can't thank that hotel enough for messing up our rooms, for providing us the vast amount of alcohol needed to act on our feelings. The moment you kissed me was the very moment you destroyed my heart and any hope I had of resisting you. Charlotte Evans, I love you more than you will ever know. I've loved you since the moment I first laid eyes on you. Will you—"

"Yes!"

"Marry me?"

"Yes, yes! A thousand times yes!" I launch myself at him, knocking Craig over, I don't care. I kiss him, pressing my body against his, then pull away, breathless. Craig slides the ring on my finger and I can't stop the tears from pouring from my eyes. Craig kisses me, then snaps a picture.

She said YES! #luckiestmanalive

LOTTIE

I hear the clattering of wood as Craig puts the crib together. The Moses basket has been set up for about a month now, and the baby won't be going into the crib immediately but trust Craig to be on the ball and ahead of the game. Every spare second he has had within the last few weeks has been dedicated to this baby.

I run a bath determined to at least attempt to shave and not look like a mammoth in case the baby comes early. I never thought I'd have to feel around to find my vagina but here we are... pregnant life.

I've packed my hospital bag and it's all ready to go. Craig has invested in a family car for us all now. He still has his van for work but we can't very well drive home with a newborn from the hospital in it. It's strange to think that my due date is a little over a month away.

Running the sponge down my arms I feel a gush. Did I just pee myself? I look into the water, did my... did my water just go?

"Craig!"

"Yeah?" I hear his muffled call from the baby's room next door.

"I think... I think my water broke."

"What?" A thud, followed by a heavy footfall and he is at the door within seconds. "Your water broke?"

"I don't know. I'm in here! I definitely felt something!"

"I'll ring the hospital." I hear him on the phone explaining the situation to the midwife on the other end. "She's not sure, she was in the bath when it happened... Yeah... ok sure... yeah, thanks, bye!"

"Better bring you in to get you checked just in case," he's already armed with a towel.

Craig drives us to the hospital, surprisingly calm.

"I hope it was my waters now and I'm not going in because the baby pressed on my bladder, how embarrassing would that be!"

"Better to be safe than sorry, babe," he waits for me to shuffle out of the car, thank God we are not waiting long. We are called in pretty quickly. The usual pee in this cup, blood pressure checks, a swab (that one is new) then a scan to see what they're dealing with.

As soon as the baby is pulled up on the screen we can easily see there is still a lot of fluid around them. Great. I peed myself and wasted the midwives' time!

I pull on my jumper, ready to leave when the doctor comes in. She is holding a chart in one hand and with the other, she reaches for me. "Let's get you set up for the night, shall we?"

"I'm sorry?"

"The swab we took shows that traces of amniotic fluid," she explains.

"Meaning, what?" Craig asks.

"Meaning that Charlotte is at risk of infection, we cannot induce you just yet, but if you go naturally we obviously won't stop it."

"So, I'm here for how long exactly?"

"Until that baby comes."

Craig and I share a concerned look, I'm moved to a semi-private room and all I can do is sit on the bed in shock. The woman on the bed next to me has a little girl. It's strange to think my little peanut will be filling one of those clear cribs soon.

"You are thirty-four-four, Charlotte, we can induce you on Wednesday if the baby is not here by then."

"Wednesday!" Craig shrieks.

"A bit earlier than expected," the doctor smiles sympathetically.

"I have nothing done!"

"You have everything done, Craig," I turn to the doctor, rolling my eyes. "You can tell this is our first, yeah?"

She smirks, "It's normal for a bit of nerves from both parents. It's a big step. Meeting your new baby."

"On Wednesday!" Craig repeats.

"Yes, batman. Wednesday."

"You will be induced on Wednesday, Charlotte, but do not be surprised if you do not have the baby until Thursday. It is your first after all and the first tends to move slowly."

"Oh no... I'm not being in labour for days at a time. No. Wednesday is the day. I'm having them then."

"What are you planning on doing, smoking them out?" Craig teases.

"I'll hold a bar of chocolate down there, if they're like me they'll come out for it."

"And if they're more like me?"

"Offer up an Xbox control."

"Touche."

Well, the past two days have been... BORING AS HELL! No one talks, they're too into their phones to bother saying hello!

Craig brought me in some books to keep me occupied and Mom, Shannon, and Tiffy have been in to visit. I've been bouncing on that giant ball for hours on end and taking the stairs every hour trying to get myself going. Nothing. Not a damn thing. Meanwhile, I've had three different roommates so far and every one of them has had their babies and left. It's my turn now!

5. am. I'm being induced at six. I can't sleep. Mainly because my latest roommate came in last night, barely put her bags on the floor and her waters broke. I can hear her shrieks coming from the labour ward right now. Our room

is right opposite those doors. It's doing nothing to help my nerves but I don't care. I'll take the pain right now. I want my baby. I want to go home. I haven't slept since I've been here!

The girls from the kitchens come up with a breakfast for me, it sort of feels like the last meal. No sign of Craig yet, he was in a blind panic last night about becoming a father today that he was halfway to Josie's before he realised he was driving in the wrong direction and had to turn back. I was wondering what took him so long to get home until he rang and explained everything to me when he eventually got in the door.

Anita is brought back to the room with a little girl, she looks knackered, yet... euphoric. It's nice to see. I'm led down the green mile within minutes of Anita's arrival.

I'm left sitting on a bed/chair thing on the doctor's arrival. This is just peachy. At least they have the radio on. I can hear the midwives' handover from the station and I'm wondering where Craig is.

"*The lazy bastard is probably still asleep!*" I say to Shannon. I need to vent. To keep my nerves calm for what is to come.

"I'm sure he is on the way, he wouldn't miss this!" Shannon replies, putting me at ease.

A doctor comes in, one I am not familiar with. He is tall and of course, he has to be attractive! Why can't I be induced by a woman? I know I attempted to shave, but for all I know I've got a comb-over going on down there! Probably patches of pubic hair remain like a warped chessboard. Ah, fuck this! Where is Craig! This is his fault!

"You should start to feel something in about half an hour," The doctor explains as he stands back up. I'm afraid to tell him I'm already feeling something. Shit, this is uncomfortable.

"You might need a second go later if this doesn't take." Want a fucking bet!

I grip the side of the bed, breathing through these waves of dull ache coursing through me. It's fine. I can do this. I can do this. Where the fuck is he?

Sweet baby Jemimah! This is coming fast.

"Help! SOS! I don't want to do this anymore!! I've changed my mind!!!!"

"You got this, boo!" Shannon replies and I want to put my hand through the screen and throat punch her. I want my mammy. How the hell did she do this twice?

Craig's head floats in the door and if I could move, I'd punch him. "It's about damn time!"

"How is mom?" A midwife asks.

I growl in reaction.

"Feeling it already? That's a good sign!"

Says fucking who? "This is sore!"

"You're not even in proper labour yet..."

"What!!!!! It gets worse?"

Craig reaches for my hand, squeezing tightly. "You can do this, baby."

"I have no fucking choice, do I!"

"You should go get something to eat while you can," Julia, my midwife says. I glance at the clock, two o'clock already? When did that happen? Craig holds onto me and guides me back to my room for dinner. They said they'll check me after. I've to be back at half two.

I manage to eat and I'm left clinging to the wall and stopping every few feet as I walk back to the labour ward.

"That's a good sign!" One of the midwives calls as she marches by me.

"Kick her in the flaps for me!" I tell Craig, who laughs and holds me tighter.

The doctor comes in to check on progress. I didn't realise

she was Freddie Krueger's sister. As soon as she puts her hand in there, I almost blackout. The tears free flow down my face and I'm inhaling the gas and air.

Wait, oh shit! No, no... Throwing my head forward I projectile vomit. After I'm done the midwife tries to hand me back the gas.

"Keep it! I don't want it!"

Craig clutches my hand tighter.

"I can't do this!" I've never felt pain like this before in my life. It's blinding. Nauseating. Please, God, make it stop! "I want the epidural!"

Julia confirms that I'm three centimeters and sends someone for the anesthesiologist. I want the drugs. I want the drugs! I WANT THE FUCKING DRUGS!!!

"Where the hell is he?" I snap, looking for the anesthesiologist.

"He should be here soon, baby. You're doing great."

"No! I want the drugs or I'm going home!"

He holds me tighter, rubbing slow soothing circles around my back. It will all be worth it soon, I keep telling myself. I can do this, I can do this... I can't fucking do this! "Craig!!!"

The anaesthetist comes in with the epidural. About damn time! I sit up, clutching onto Craig for dear life.

"Tell me when the contraction finishes," my saviour instructs.

"I will If it ever does!" As soon as one contraction starts to ease, I'm blasted with another. There is no break in here. This is hell. I'm going to die. My fanny is going to explode. I want my mammy!!!!

Suddenly a wave of bliss hits, the pain stops. Oh holy God, thank you!

Craig settles me on the bed, then I'm handed a waiver to sign. I couldn't give a rat's furry ass what it says, the pain stopped! It stopped! I barely remember signing my name. This is bliss, yes! Bliss! Thank God! Thank God for the person who invented that epidural. Oh heaven!

I'm that zoned out, I don't know what is going on in the room, I hear Craig speaking with Julia but I can't take in what they're saying. There is someone else in the room. A nurse. I think I vaguely remember agreeing to let a student in for learning purposes? I don't care. The pain is gone.

"Eight centimeters!" Julia beams.

"That fast?" Craig gawkes.

"That can happen, as soon as the body can relax it just... opens. Not long now, Charlotte, you're doing great!"

Julia goes on her lunch while I'm still stoned off my face. Yay bliss, I could nap, maybe... I tilt my head up to look at Craig, he is so handsome. How did I get so lucky?

Holy mother of all things unholy what sort of fresh hell is this? That uncomfortable tightening is coming back. Oh no. No! No! No! I got the drugs! I'm not supposed to feel this! Begone Satan!

Gripping the sides of the bed, I start to breathe. I haven't a clue what I'm doing. Copying what I've seen the women do in one born every minute. My first class was today! I'm missing it by being in labour early. Why does this baby hate me? Just breathe, Lottie, breathe... I look back at Craig who is still talking to the nurse. That bastard did this to me!!

I need the drugs! I got a bad dose! I need a fucking exorcism! Help!!!!!

"I need to push!" I growl.

"You can't need to already, you only got the epidural an hour ago," the matron dismisses the idea entirely, not even checking.

"I know I have nothing to compare it to! But I'm telling you, I need to fucking push!"

She doesn't so much as move to me and keeps talking with the student. Are you shitting me?

Julia walks back in, "Julia!!!!!! I NEED TO PUSH!!"

She walks towards me, hiking the blanket up, then spins and puts on an apron and gloves.

"Ok, Charlotte, when I tell you to push, you push...ok?"

"I told you I needed to push!!!!" I snap at the matron. The first push, Craig looks down, beaming. "They have so much hair!" The second push, I feel some relief. Almost there, Lottie. Craig grips me tighter. "Come on, baby. Almost there. You're doing so good." Third push, I glance down to see a tiny body land on the bed.

"You did it, baby! You did it! I'm so proud of you!" Craig brushes away the tears from his eyes while the midwives clean down the baby.

"What is it?" I ask, flooded with sheer relief.

"You tell us," The matron holds up this beautiful little person, the umbilical cord blocks my view, so I use a finger to push it out of the way. Craig is still crying, pretending that he's not by turning to face the wall and rubbing at his face.

"A boy!" I beam. "We have a boy!"

"Thank you," Craig leans down, kissing me and nuzzling into my neck. "Thank you for him, you did so well, baby, so well."

I'm handed our little man. Craig leans over both of us, kissing my head every few seconds, his hands trembling.

"Ethan?" I ask, looking up at Craig.

"Ethan," he confirms. Pulling his phone from his pocket he snaps a picture to send to Josie and mom. Then I hand him Ethan to do skin to skin while I get sewn back together.

Ethan has a little grunt so the midwives take him to SCBU. As soon as I'm patched up and fed tea and toast, Craig wheels me down to our baby.

He has a feeding tube in, the midwives told us that Ethan's suck has not developed yet so he will need that until he can take a bottle or latch onto my breast.

I snap a picture for Shannon and Tiffy.

Screw it!

Say hello to our little man xxx

EPILOGUE

" So, yeah my dad has taken Jamie for the weekend. Jay and I will pick you guys up on the way," Tiffy says.

"That's fine I could use a break from the kids."

"Doing your nut in?"

"Something like that, that and work..."

"Please Cry me a river, Mrs bestselling author, gag me with a spoon, your life is perfect."

"It is, isn't it!"

"Hold on a sec... JAMIE, PUT THAT DOWN NOW! I swear he is every bit of his father!"

"Troublemaker?" I snort.

"Without a doubt!"

"I know the feeling, actually it's a little too quiet here... Ellie!"

"Mommy?" her little auburn head sticks out of the sitting room. She is two years Ethan's junior.

"Where are Ethan and dad?"

"Outside."

"Are they dressed? We're going to the park in a sec."

"Yep, I saw them."

"Good, grab your coat for me, good girl."

"OK!"

"I'll let you go," I say to Tiffy.

"OK, text you later."

I know they say the time goes fast but it really does fly. It seems like we only brought Ethan home from the hospital yesterday, my baby boy just turned six. I left my job in the pharmacy and with the new time on my hands, I wrote out our story, mine and Craig's. It took a few tries but I eventually got a publisher and now I work from home.

Grabbing the car keys I help Ellie zip up her coat. As much as I love the kids, I can't wait for a break away this weekend, back to the place where it all started, the hotel that Nick got married in. It's an annual thing every year Jason, Tiffy, Craig, and I drive up to the hotel for a long weekend, abandoning the kids with Josie or my mom. It's a way to guarantee some alone time for us adults and also catch up, well for Tiffy and me anyway. Jason and Craig see each other all the time.

Their business is doing well, what used to be five contracts on the go is now fifteen and twenty.

Michael just got released from prison, but he is not allowed anywhere near me or my family. After the state Craig left him in, I doubt we'll ever have to worry about him showing his face again.

"They were just here!" Ellie whines. The boys are always doing this, I might as well have three kids, not two.

"Craig, Ethan, come on guys, let's go!"

"Mommy," Ellie points towards the road and it's then that I see them, it's not like I could miss them. Two little Spidermen, or should I say one big Spidey and a little spider.

"No Batman today?" I ask Craig.

"Suit's in the wash."

"Come on then, Spidey, you're driving." I clip Ellie into her car seat while the big spider helps the little spider into his.

"All set?" Craig asks.

"All set," I put my hand on his, feeling his wedding band through the costume.

"Two Spiderman, one Princess, and a Queen," Craig beams, glancing back at the kids.

"Two Spiderman, one Princess, one Queen, and a peanut."

"What?"

"I don't see any peanuts, mommy," Ellie frowns.

"Me neither," Ethan looks at the floor.

"That's because it's in my belly."

Craig gawkes at me, "are you serious?"

"Yeah, your pull-out game is weak."

"Are we going to the park now?" Ethan asks.

"Come on, daddy," Ellie demands.

"I'm going, I'm going," Craig buckles up his seat belt and I pass him the scan of the baby. "Peanut," he beams, looking down at the image in his hands.

"Peanut," I grin at him as he slides the picture into his wallet. He leans in kissing me, the kids' audible disgust makes us both laugh.

"Who's ready for an adventure?" Craig asks.

"I am!" Ethan cheers.

"Me too!" Ellie beams.

"Mommy?" Craig looks at me, eyes sparkling. I gripped his hand tightly and smile, "always."

Coming soon

Screw you, too!

Printed in Great Britain
by Amazon